D1528161

Diary of an
Accidental Nursing Home Aide

Linda Lewis

Diary of an
Accidental Nursing Home Aide

Stories of Life and Death during COVID-19

LINDA LEWIS

Linda Lewis

DEDICATION

For my mother, Christel Rostek Mattern,
whose story ended much too soon.

Linda Lewis

Linda Lewis

AKNOWLEDGEMENTS

I would like to thank my mother's friends and neighbors at Trillium, including Barbara and Bob Gilliland, Clara Green, and Brenda Ratcliff. Your selfless care and assistance leading up to my mom's illness was appreciated. Special thanks to the members of the St. Mark's Lutheran Church choir, especially Sherryl Sheets-May, who inspired my mom with her musical talent, and Betsy Becker, for being a wonderful friend and providing rides to church and choir practice. Thanks to Rita Selle-Grider for her faith, leadership, and love of all things German, and to Betty Pingrey, my mother's first childhood friend when she first came to this country. Many thanks to my friend, beta reader, and encourager-in-chief, Pamela Denius Gillum, for pushing me to get this project done. Also, to my readers here and abroad who like my stories and write flattering reviews, I appreciate you! Finally, I am forever grateful to Tim Lewis, my one true love, who supported my brief career as a nurse's aide during the pandemic. Your love and patience as my husband and friend mean everything.

WELCOME

If you don't like Mary Poppins, then you probably won't like me.

"Hello, hello! Tell me something good!" I burst through the door and greeted my first patient with a smile, a hug, and a spoon full of sugar. We were making rounds, checking temperatures during the days of COVID-19.

"What is it with you, girl?" asked a coworker. "Why are you so happy all the time?" Gosh, if she only knew. "I'm going to start calling you Mary Poppins!"

I raised an eyebrow and grinned. "Oh, and why it that?"

"Because you're practically perfect in every way." A blessing and a curse to be sure…

Linda Lewis

PREFACE AND DISCLAIMER

Please enjoy this preface and disclaimer... possibly the most thorough and most amusing you will ever read.

Much of this story is wildly fictionalized, washed in the fanciful prose and self-deprecating humor that are the hallmark of my writing style. I am not really Mary Poppins and I cannot do magic, although some of the old people I've cared for would swear otherwise.

This work depicts some actual events in the life of the author (me), as truthfully as recollection permits or can be verified by research. Some events were told to me by people who gave me permission to include their stories here. Occasionally dialog consistent with a character or nature of the person speaking has been supplemented. All Personally Identifiable Information (PID) meets the De-Identification Standard for Section 164.514 of the HIPAA Privacy Rule. Any resemblance to actual people, living or dead, is purely coincidental. Factual material is drawn from a variety of sources, including published materials, interviews, and the State Long-term Care Ombudsman's office. All are appropriately cited, just like they made us do in college.

For dramatic and narrative purposes, this work contains fictionalized scenes and characters, including some old favorites, like Neil Lipman, Janet from the unemployment office in Petoskey, and Kelly the manager from the Charlevoix Boat Basin. Other characters and events are composites I created to help move the story forward. The Coronavirus pandemic and the death of my mother, however, really happened.

Cambridge Memorial and Saint Alidocious Hospitals (pronounced al-i-doh-shuhs) exist only in my imagination. Any medical information from an imaginary hospital should not be considered factual and is not a substitute for professional medical advice. Please, if you have symptoms, see a real doctor. Cherry Tree Old Folks Home is a loosely knitted tapestry of all the care facilities, from south Florida to northern Michigan, where I have devoted my time over the past twenty years. One previously published story is reprinted in this text because it is so wondrous and inspiring it's worth repeating. Her name was Sophie.

As a former hospice direct care volunteer in three states, I have a shoebox full of letters and cards from families whose loved ones I cared for, *and cared about— a* Charter Captain, a Holocaust survivor, and an engineer retired from Boeing with three patents pending. Hospice provided me with training to care for a dying person's emotional and spiritual needs, but I never received the instruction to be an adequate aide. While my desire to serve during the pandemic was genuine, the rigors of providing hands-on care— the lifting, transferring, and repositioning of heavy humans was out of reach. Kudos to my coworkers on the front lines for all you do. I will be forever grateful to those who gave me a chance to try.

For anyone who was friends with my beloved mother, it's true that she died during the days of COVID-19, however, she never contracted the virus; her diagnosis was far more grave. This memoir tells the story of the last months of her life, where her German heritage, kindness, and generosity of spirit continued to shine through. Finally, my mom was a huge promoter of my books. She would be glad you purchased a copy and would encourage you to share it with a friend.

So grab your umbrella and jump with me into a magical sidewalk chalk drawing, where you'll find laughter, tears, and an unexpected, bittersweet reunion.

*These are the 18 HIPAA Identifiers that are considered personally identifiable information. This information can be used to identify, contact, or locate a single person or can be used with other sources to identify a single individual. When personally identifiable information is used in conjunction with one's physical or mental health or condition, health care, or one's payment for that health care, it becomes Protected Health Information (PHI): Name, Address (all geographic subdivisions smaller than state, including street address, city county, and zip code) All elements (except years) of dates related to an individual (including birthdate, admission date, discharge date, date of death, and exact age if over 89), Telephone numbers, Fax number, Email address, Social Security Number, Medical record number, Health plan beneficiary number, Account number, Certificate or license number, Vehicle identifiers and serial numbers, including license plate numbers, Device identifiers and serial numbers, Web URL, Internet Protocol (IP) Address, Finger or voice print, Photographic image - Photographic images are not limited to images of the face, and Any other characteristic that could uniquely identify the individual. If a communication contains any of these identifiers, or parts of the identifier, such as initials, the data is to be considered "identified". To be considered "de-identified", ALL the 18 HIPAA Identifiers must be removed from the data set. This includes all dates, such as surgery dates, all voice recordings, and all photographic images.

Linda Lewis

Christel

I never expected my mom to end up in a nursing home, and I never imagined myself working in one, either. The photo on the cover is the two of us in 2019, shopping at Oakland Greenhouse, where she had to touch every geranium before choosing two. She was particular and liked things a certain way, and I suppose I'm like that, too. The sun was intensely bright that morning, which is why we were both wearing sunglasses. We were not trying to be cool…

My mom, Christel Rostek Mattern, came to America from Germany at age eleven, four years after the end of World War II. She used to tell stories about the bombings, and how she ran with her classmates to a nearby shelter when the sirens blew. On the day her family's home was destroyed, they sorted through the rubble, salvaged what they could, and moved on. With memories of war so traumatic and profound, her identity, and to some extent her allegiance, would always be to her motherland.

In 1960, she graduated with a degree in English from Temple University. I was born two years later, the oldest of three with two younger brothers. She earned her master's degree from The Ohio State University, and taught school for 35 years. Even at age 82, she was energetic, opinionated, and did the crossword puzzle (in ink) every day. Everything was fine... until it wasn't.

In July of 2020, four months into the COVID-19 epidemic, my mom was taken to the emergency room by EMS. She had fallen several times earlier that week trying to get out of bed. Finally, the paramedics convinced her she needed to get some help. She always told me she was fine... that these falls were caused by various different things. Once was due to the lotion the home health aide rubbed on her feet; an emollient cream that made them slippery. We solved that problem together with some skidproof hospital socks and a door mat with some grip placed at her bedside. Another time it was the adjustable bed that didn't quite lift her high enough to step off and get her balance. We considered the options together and decided that rails and grab bars were a solid fix. When that didn't help either, I found a bed that would actually stand her strait up in the morning until her feet touched the floor. It was $3500; I told her it was worth it.

"Yes, Mom, it's a lot of money, but you can certainly afford it, and it's way cheaper than moving to a nursing home. If we can work this out, you can stay here at the condo and be independent for as long as you like." She agreed, as we sat at the dining room table working on a puzzle of the Schloss Neuschwanstein, a castle in Southern Bavaria near the small town where she lived. The table was from our old house on Dorsetshire where my brothers and I grew up. It was the center of holiday dinners, the place where our mom served traditional meals, always using her 'good' china and silverware. We were little then, and being cared for— not the other way around. Time goes by fast.

It was a Sunday. When the emergency room at Cambridge Memorial Hospital called, I wasn't alarmed. My mom had been to this hospital once before when she stumbled on a sidewalk taking pictures uptown, but never for a true emergency. The nurse explained they were doing some tests to learn why she was falling so much.

Was it balance? Her blood pressure medicine, perhaps? A mini stroke? Maybe it was just old age, or the first sign of dementia setting in. My mom was *healthy as a horse*, as we used to say in the old days. When all the tests came back normal, I wasn't satisfied. Something happened to my mom; we had to figure out what it was.

My mom was the social center of her community, hosting Monday night scrapbooking events at her house that always included fresh baked goodies and coffee for her friends. She taught jewelry making, and as a photographer with a keen eye for all things that bloom, she taught the Monday night gals how to make notecards with photographs, sharing the secrets of how to get the discount on developing film at Walgreens and CVS. Her geraniums were among the nicest on her block; she was beauty personified.

My mother was a force, (a German!), not a sick person. A classic extrovert, she was buoyant and vivacious. Known for her kindness and generosity, she never showed up empty handed, and loved baking brownies— with or without nuts. She volunteered at the state parks and sold her jewelry at a prestigious art gallery in town, (although she gave away as many bracelets as she sold.) She never missed a parade, a festival, or a fundraiser at the local

B.O.E. She participated in the annual condo association garage sale, not to make an extra buck, but to greet and visit with her neighbors returning from their winter homes in Florida. Even with a walker, she never missed choir practice. Thank God this episode was just a bump in the road, a blip on the radar screen of her exceptional life, I thought to myself. She would work hard at physical therapy and return home to her geraniums and the hens and chickens in clay pots by the porch. It's good to be an extrovert, especially in the hospital, where winning over the staff would work in her favor. I had peace about this.

Unlike my mom, I am a solid introvert. I'm friends with more dogs than humans. I order my groceries online and prefer Netflix over conversation. When COVID-19 put an abrupt end to shopping at stores, I was already enjoying free second day delivery with Amazon Prime. (My mom was both delighted and mystified when a blue and white package showed up on her doorstep, whether it was a new puzzle, winter socks, or clip-on ice cleats! I'm still not sure she understood how it all worked and I never tried to explain. It was just fun to make the magic happen, just like Mary...)

Old people were sealed off in their houses, disinfecting their door handles, and watching the governor on TV every day at 2pm. We talked on the phone before the big show, my mom keeping track of the numbers and knowing which counties were in danger of a surge. The social isolation of COVID-19 was hard on her. While she had lots of visitors socially distanced on the other side of her storm door, it never fulfilled her need to be surrounded by people. My contentment for staying home in my pajamas with my husband and four little dogs made it even less likely that I would venture out to the front lines of a global pandemic, caring for old people at high risk for the deadly virus.

COVID-19 meant restricted visits at Cambridge Memorial. One visitor was allowed, but not in the ER, and only in her room once she got in there, which could take an hour or a day, no one could say. The visitor had to be the *only* visitor during her hospital stay and could only stay a half hour. Even on a different day, only the visitor from the first day could go in. My brother and I would need to evaluate the terms wisely. I could not believe that after four long months, the virus had not been contained and there was no end in sight. With nothing to indicate otherwise, the doctor said she was probably just out of shape from lack of exercise and released her to a rehabilitation center to get better. She was less than an hour from me, and since she was only going to be there a short while, the distance was manageable. I hoped some of the restrictions would be lifted so I could see her.

That's when the rules changed. Care Centers everywhere were posting new fatalities daily, and the numbers were soaring! Once COVID-19 was inside a facility there was little stopping it and scores of old people perished. The virus was being transmitted from nurses who attended weddings, to patients in their care. Aides who masked up at work but otherwise ignored the guidelines were getting residents sick without knowing it. Even family members who were asymptomatic but eventually tested positive, were unwittingly killing their loved ones.

The first time I saw my mom was at a window visit at the rehab... an impossible substitute for giving hugs and sharing German chocolate and candy. Even small talk seemed pointless through the glass. "Mom, out here! Look out the window! It's me!" Standing in rainwater and weeds up to my ankles, I waved at her. The glare on the glass made it difficult to see in. With my face pressed against the window (that silly thing we did as kids), I hoped for a laugh or a smile. When she came closer, I noticed she was still in her nightgown— it was the middle of the afternoon! *What kind of place is this,* I thought to myself? I made a mental note to find out what was going on here. How could a care facility be so lax and inefficient? Are those aides sitting around looking at their phones and texting their boyfriends while my mom isn't even dressed? How hard can their jobs possibly be?" How hard, indeed...

I shouted through the glass to the physical therapist who was steadying her with a gait belt. He said she was trying hard, but not making much progress. I figured she was exhausted; she had been through a lot. "What is she being treated for? Can you tell me her diagnosis?" He shrugged. There had to be a diagnosis, right? You couldn't very well help someone get well if you didn't know what was wrong with them in the first place.

"Hey, hi..." I said when someone picked up the phone. I was calling the rehab from the parking lot. "Thanks so much for taking good care of my mom," I said through a smile that was in no way sincere. "Must be a crazy time for you all, with COVID-19 and all that." (If I'm trying to win someone over or need a favor, it often helps to slip into a southern accent so people will think I'm nicer than I really am. It works if you get picked up for speeding, too.)

"So, hey… I know y'all are busy and all, but if you can help me, I sure would appreciate it. Is there any way you can find out my mother's diagnosis? When she came over from Cambridge Memorial, what did they say was wrong with her?" Hold music, long pause. A crackling sound made me think this call would end without getting what I came for.

"Right. So we never got the bundle from the hospital," said a nurse in a mechanical tone.

"The bundle?" I replied. Was this a thing?

"Right. The bundle is the paperwork that has all her test results and the treatment notes that were entered every day when somebody checked on her."

"So the doctors, the nurses… they would have notated something about her care. Is that right?"

"Yes, exactly," she continued, a keyboard clicking away in the background.

"So if nobody has those notes, and nobody knows her diagnosis, how are you guys able to help her? How can she get better if there is no information?"

The rehab center was treating my mom without knowing what was wrong! I was outraged, ready to march in there and straighten these people out. I would not accept that level of incompetence and laziness, not if it was one of my little dogs at the vet, much less my own mother! I was about to unleash my frustration over the virus and my mom's mysterious illness onto the folks at the rehab. I wasn't sure if it would help or not.

"Tell me where I can get those medical records, so you can start doing your job and taking care of my mom.

Diary of an Accidental Nursing Home Aide

Linda Lewis

The Bundle

Saint Alidocious Hospital (pronounced al-i-doh-shuhs) is a leading medical center. Over time, it has swallowed up many of the smaller hospitals in the region, including Cambridge Memorial. The main hospital, plus the old additions, the new additions, and the addition of a cutting-edge cancer research center were all connected by a maze of catwalks and underground tunnels— a city within a city. It covered 170 acres and had 1400 beds on the main campus alone. It was an intimidating site, dwarfing every structure in its shadow. Saint Alidocious was the keeper of the magic bundle that hopefully had information about my mom's diagnosis. The real question was, would it help her get better, or was it too late?

Diary of an Accidental Nursing Home Aide

From the parking garage I spotted a glass entranceway and a security desk flanked by two stone-faced guards. I hated how COVID-19 was making nice people feel like criminals. A long line of visitors was waiting to get in. I knew from the governor's daily address that ICU beds were filling fast. I wondered how many of these folks had loved ones that were dying inside— a chilling thought. Prevention protocols were changing daily, and the CDC was scrambling to contain the virus. The nurses at the desk worked quickly while the guards looked on. Each visitor had their temperature taken and was screened with a battery of questions.

"Have you had a fever greater than 100.4 as measured by an oral thermometer?"

"Shortness of breath, trouble breathing, or a cough?

"Sore throat, chills, or loss of taste or smell?"

"Headaches? Muscle aches? Nausea, diarrhea, vomiting?"

There was no way for them to know I had been living in a bubble long before the virus began.

"Have you traveled out of state? For work or for play? Where did you go? How long did you stay?"

"Have you been to a wedding, a funeral, a park? A concert, the zoo, alone or apart?

"I couldn't imagine how these nurses spent an entire day wrapped in plastic gowns, a mask, and face shield, asking the same questions again and again. They had to be miserable. The interrogation was daunting, but I knew Saint Alidocious had a job to do. It was for everyone's safety.

"I actually just popped in to use the ladies' room," I whispered to the guard. "My mamma is in the car waiting. If y'all would be so kind, I would just be a minute." A man in uniform can never resist a pretty girl with a southern accent, practically perfect in every way, at least where fake accents are concerned.

Like a super sleuth on a critical mission, I dashed around the corner and into a little cove by the restrooms, waiting for a group of workers in scrubs to pass by. With my head down and my mask in place, I stepped out and followed them unnoticed. I took the red concourse past the orange information desk, through the yellow lobby, and around the new blue cancer wing. I slipped cautiously past the blue elevators, careful to avoid eye contact, and through the green cafeteria where a security guard eating a cheeseburger glared at me. I knew I wasn't supposed to be there and didn't want my mission to end before I reached the elusive Office of Medical Records. I could not afford to get caught! A sign on a post pointed the way to the purple area just ahead. It was the last color at the end of the medical rainbow. A nurse stepped into the elevator ahead of me. "What floor?" she asked.

"Basement… Medical Records," I mumbled.

"Do you have an appointment?"

"I do… sort of. I called first."

She expertly tapped the button with her elbow, as if COVID-19 protocols had become second nature.

The office of Medical Records was dimly lit by a single fluorescent light overhead, and the glass receptionist window was vacant. There was a chair in the corner and a stack of dated magazines gathering dust. "What can I do for you?" said a voice. "I'll be there in just one minute."

"I called ahead. I need my mom's paperwork… the bundle… Christel Mattern. She was in Cambridge Memorial a week ago, came in through the ER." A lady stepped out from behind a closed door. She said in a pleasant voice, "My name is Janet, you can come with me." She seemed strangely familiar. Janet led the way to a cubicle at the end of a long hall. She was a Black lady well into her sixties with a round face and a cameo pin on her blouse. On her metal desk sat a leggy, dry Poinsettia, probably left over from Christmas, a small stone cross, and an "IN" box crowded with paperwork— not a good sign.

"Yes, I'm the one you talked to. Did you get all the documents?" Her demeanor was sympathetic. I had everything but her healthcare Power of Attorney. I explained the circumstances. "When people are sick, it's hard to keep track of every detail. Let me make a call."

Janet picked up the phone, called the rehab center, and asked for a woman named Rita. Janet faxed over a document and asked Rita to have my mom sign it, giving consent for me to receive her records. Within minutes, my mom's faint signature arrived via fax. Janet took a business card from a plastic holder on her desk, handed me a heavy envelope, then stood up indicating our meeting was over. "If you need anything else, just call." As I began to walk away, Janet said in a soft voice, "I'll be praying for you." I wondered if she knew something I didn't.

I walked away with a pile of papers two-inches thick. At a time when everything else was going wrong, a daunting trip to Saint Alidocious turned out okay. I took this as affirmation that God was on my side, and would facilitate the tricky parts as I tried to help my mom get well. I'm glad Janet was praying for me.

Diary of an Accidental Nursing Home Aide

On the phone, my mom's voice was week. She had been at the rehab for ten days. "How are you doing with your exercises, Mom? I hear you're working really hard. That's good, you know, because getting stronger is the key to going home again." It was a pep talk, but I was being sincere. We were well into campaign season; the election was four months away. I knew she had already voted by absentee ballot. She was fastidious about those types of things, and never missed a detail.

"How 'bout this campaign, Mom… what a mess, right?" I couldn't get her interested in anything I said. "How 'bout the governor's press conference yesterday? I really miss Dr. Amy. (Amy Acton M.D. was the much-loved Department of Health Director who had just resigned.)

She quietly repeated, "Yes, Dr. Amy."

"I think people tune in just to watch her," I said, pretending it was like old times when we talked on the phone about everything. Dr. Amy was kind and pretty, with long chestnut hair and a warm smile. Her daily presence was reassuring as COVID-19 infections continued to climb. Watching the reports had become a 'thing,' with folks gathering around their TV's each day, some sipping wine as Dr. Amy presented updates about the virus; her imitable spirit offered words of hope and encouragement. My mom used to watch every day, but now she slept through the whole show. Whatever had happened to her, the event that caused such a radical change so quickly, gave me a sense of urgency, a feeling that there wasn't much time.

Seated at my own dining room table and armed with a pot of coffee, I divided the bundle into sections: tests and test results, treatment notes, medications, referrals, and recommendations. I made a page with columns where I wrote down her vital signs and pills she was given during her hospital stay. I made lists of symptoms and terms that appeared in the documents consistently and looked up the definitions of words I didn't know. I concluded she was suffering from delirium which, thank God, is treatable. One of her neighbors suggested she might have had a stroke, and her cleaning lady said it might be a rare form of hydrocephalus; that someone in her family had the exact same symptoms. I was open to all possibilities. I called to remind her that I was working on this… that I was thinking of her and not giving up.

Diary of an Accidental Nursing Home Aide

Linda Lewis

Human Warehousing

"Christel, Christel, wake up, wake up!" The aide was a young man, shouting at her, trying to rouse her from what was hopefully just a deep sleep. "Wake up, Christel... it's your daughter!"

Why couldn't he wake her? What the heck is going on at this place? Oh my God, is she gone? Is my mother dead?! The aide didn't seem alarmed and advised me to call again later. This was not the right place for her. But for such a short stay while she got her strength back, I would deal with it, even if it meant crashing through the COVID-19 restrictions and chasing the administrator with a pointed stick until I got some answers. Nobody was accountable.

What did these people do all day? I called back, this time to talk to the director.

"Did you get the email? The email from Medical Records?" An unpleasant voice came bellowing through the phone in reply. It was Kelly the administrator, a stout middle-aged woman, with thick round glasses and a face like a bulldog. I didn't like her, and the feeling was mutual. "All you had to do was click on the link the hospital sent yesterday. Janet at Saint Alidocious emailed it to you… I was standing right there!"

"I don't always check my email," she muttered.

"WHAT?!"

"I'm the administrant. I don't work on the medical side."

"Kelly," I was livid. "Are you running a care center or selling Avon? Lives are depending on you to do the right thing!" I was weary, too depleted to do a southern accent, but not to the point of giving up. "My mom is failing. Something happened to her. She is a loud, outgoing, German woman! She does not stay in bed all day in her nightgown! My mom takes charge and gets things done. She is a force, a teacher, and she's failing, and you have no idea why! Open you're damn email!"

"I'll check with someone on the medical side. I don't work on the medical side."

I continued to tear through the bundle, grouping symptoms and googling possible causes, comparing the search results with notes from the hospital. Why do people turn to the internet to try to diagnose themselves or their loved ones? Is it because we think we are doctors and we know everything? Is it to minimize the value of long years of education and to usurp their authority like petulant children who demand their own way? Or is it because we are desperate, frustrated, and actually give a damn about whether our people live or die?

"I want my mom to see a neurologist." Kelly, are you listening to me?" She was having a snack, something crunchy. Based on my research, my mother's symptoms were consistent with a problem in her brain or spinal column. I decided that's the direction we would go. I would have gladly turned the role of doctor/scientist over to someone who was more qualified, but no one was interested. Her primary care physician was sympathetic, but stated he couldn't visit patients at the rehab. They had their own doctor to provide care, who was actually a nurse practitioner, who was frequently absent from work, and never available for questions. There was no one.

Diary of an Accidental Nursing Home Aide

"They can get her in the last week of September," Kelly stated. By now it was August. That was six weeks away.

"Not acceptable." How does this woman live with herself? My mom couldn't hold even a brief conversation on the phone, and our porch visits were like sitting with an old person who was disappearing more each day. "No, the end of September won't do. Get on the phone, make some calls, and make this happen sooner. This is the most important thing you're going to do today, so you better get started now."

What mattered so much to me mattered little to her. I was standing firm to be my mom's truest advocate. The administrant was content to collect a check every month to cover the cost of warehousing her. She got paid whether they had the bundle or not, and it didn't matter if my mom got the care she needed. When she died, a new irrelevant old person would be warehoused in her place. The rehab, the administrant, and all her complicit team members could sleep well at night knowing they would always get paid for doing as little as possible. Were they hardened to the gravity of death, or did my mom just end up in the worst facility ever? There is no way every nursing home could be this bad, or so I thought. If I could just sit in her room and talk with her, I could reassure her that things would get better, and make her smile, and bring her a nice sandwich from Shorties. But I would never see the inside of her room until the last day. I groaned, exhausted. Though I had just tested negative for COVID-19, the virus and all its restrictions were killing me.

I bought her some nice clothes from Kohl's for her birthday, some transitional pieces, and warmer things for fall. New outfits can cure practically anything, and my mom liked to look her best. This would be wonderful, I thought, as I reached for the huge, colorful gift bag on the passenger seat beside me. She would have some pretty things to wear at the rehab, and some nice outfits for when she got home. Her neighbors and friends from choir practice would be waiting. The nursing home had been dressing her in someone else's clothing. I was aghast. Were these the wardrobes of people who had passed on and no longer needed the stained and tattered outfits she was wearing? Were the aides stealing her good clothes and taking them home to wear themselves? Or was the place so disorganized that her clothes were simply never laundered and returned?

I met my mom at the neurology office two days later. A rehab center van transported her to a Saint Alidocious

Diary of an Accidental Nursing Home Aide

Medical Campus outside Cambridge where they did outpatient procedures and testing. She was pushed in a wheelchair to the front door by an aide who was covered in cheap tattoos and smoking a cigarette. Dressed in someone else's big, faded blouse, my mom had no idea where we were, but was happily surprised to see me. The neurologist was thorough and kind, with a poker face that revealed nothing. She ordered the original test results from Medical Records, scheduled a brain MRI, then a second MRI with contrast two weeks later. I was encouraged by the doctor's attention to detail and professionalism. The neurosurgeons at Saint Alidocious were among the best in the world. Whatever the results, I was sure they could help.

Linda Lewis

Crisis Point

Two weeks passed. I dropped my husband off at the repair shop where his car had been worked on that day. As I drove off, the vehicle ahead of me threw a stone from the gravel parking lot up onto my windshield, leaving a good size chip. It was the story of my life these days. I took a sip from some day-old Mountain Dew that was still in my cup holder. A cloud of dust blinded me; it was so thick I could taste it. I turned on my high beams hoping I could see clearly. *Just what I need... just one more thing to deal with.* I was exhausted from fighting with Kelly at the rehab, and fatigued from waiting to hear my mom's results. At least it wasn't a crack. My back hurt, and I was getting a migraine. I hardly slept at night, and sweat was pouring off my face. Why was it so damned hot outside? It

27

was September, for Pete's sake! Even the weather was getting on my nerves! I could not handle one more bad thing. And then my phone rang. I bounced down an uneven curb and into rush hour traffic; the chipped turned into a long crack clear across the glass.

"I have your mother's test results. Are you someplace we can talk?" It was the neurologist, the call I was dreading and also waiting for.

"There is a mass on your mother's brain. We won't know whether it's benign or malignant without a biopsy, but I can tell you that it is aggressive and fast growing." I quickly accessed the imaginary stack of files I'd been compiling in my brain, sifted through the relevant data, and knew it had to be a glioblastoma. My mom had a brain tumor.

Oh, my God... Oh, my God. My mouth turned dry as a gravel parking lot and my hands were tingling. I needed to find a place to pull off. There was probably an old Xanax somewhere in my purse. I was having a panic attack.

"I can't say for a fact that it's a glioblastoma," said the doctor, "but given her age and the rate of growth, it is the most likely cause of her symptoms. I'll send a referral to an oncologist at the Saint Alidocious Neurology Center. He's very good. They'll contact you to schedule a biopsy if that's the direction you decide to go."

"A biopsy of what? Her brain?" My hope was dwindling fast, and it was getting harder to breathe.

"It's a common procedure. Sometimes it's even done as an outpatient."

"So she needs brain surgery to find out whether she needs brain surgery?"

"Essentially yes."

"She is going to die, isn't she."

"Think about a biopsy and we'll take it from there."

I braked, swerved, and drove across three lanes of traffic. In a Taco Bell parking lot I googled glioblastoma. Not only was it lethal and fast growing, it made its own blood supply, allowing it to feed off itself as it devoured the brain— *my mother's brain.* The tumor was located in the very center, in the basil ganglia region. That explained why she was falling so much, and why she wasn't making any progress in physical therapy.

"The basil ganglia refer to a group of subcortical nuclei responsible primarily for motor control, as well as other roles such as motor learning, executive functions and behaviors, and emotions. Proposed more than two

decades ago, the classical basal ganglia model shows how information flows through two pathways with opposing effects for the proper execution of movement.... Disruption of the basal ganglia network forms the basis for several movement disorders. This article provides a comprehensive account of basal ganglia functional anatomy and chemistry and the major pathophysiological changes underlying disorders of movement."

Functional Neuroanatomy of the Basal Ganglia, Jose L. Lanciego, et al, www.ncib.nlm.nih.gov, 2012 Cold spring Harbor Laboratory Press

I'm not sure she ever understood her diagnosis or how it was related to the problems she was having. She agreed to a biopsy, then days later refused. She was confused and emotional. She was my take-charge Mom who could no longer take charge or comprehend the impact of her choices. It was just a year earlier that she announced, at age 81, that she wanted an iPhone and she wanted me to teach her to use it. She was always a prolific reader, often powering through two or three books a week, some in her native German. She knew the names of every state flower, and the names of every player on the Ohio State football team. My mom was impossibly smart, a lifelong student, fully engaged. If anyone could learn to use a smart phone, it was her.

Since her time at the hospital, plus her weeks in rehab, her posting and texting skills had grown rusty. I knew she had friends on Facebook that were waiting to hear from her. We sat companionably, weeks before her diagnosis, on the covered porch outside the main entrance at the rehab, taking advantage of that brief interval where people could visit face to face. She was in a wheelchair on the opposite side of a small table to ensure social distancing. An activities aide with a sour disposition hovered to make sure there was no hugging.

"Go ahead and press the home button on the bottom, Mom. That will turn on your phone and you'll see all your apps. I looked over my shoulder to make sure the coast was clear, then reached for her phone and turned it on.

"There you go, Mom," I said in the calming voice of a third-grade teacher, as I handed back her iPhone. You have eight apps on your home page. You recognize your home page, right?" Under the awning, the morning sun was blinding. Between her tinted glasses and homemade cotton mask I couldn't read her expression.

"You've got the Channel 10 news app on the left… it's the dark blue one!" By now I was talking through a pretend smile and choking back tears. "You remember Dominic Tiberi, right? From the pool when we all used to go swimming in the summer? When we used to play water volleyball, and Marco Polo, and eat Pixy Stix from the snack bar? Well, now he's the Sports Director there. Isn't that fantastic? Go ahead and click on the app." She nodded to be polite, but I sensed that nothing registered. "And look at this, Mom… see the little red circle in the corner of your Facebook app? You have eleven notifications! That is fantastic! Should we click on it and see who's read your posts?"

She watched without any understanding or curiosity about an activity she once enjoyed so much. She was dozing off, but I pressed on, fully believing if I explained it well enough her phone would make sense again, and we could pick up where we left off, commenting on pictures posted by friends from the old neighborhood. I patiently reviewed Liking, commenting, sharing photos, and writing posts. In her featured photos there were colorful images of puzzles she had done.

"Click on the one of the castle, Mom! It looks like it got several Likes!"

She sat quietly, so unlike her normal, talkative self. I offered her a small cherry Gatorade; the activities girl scowled. She carefully placed the plastic bottle to her mouth, took a small sip, and began to cough. My mom was choking, struggling to swallow, and coughing some more. What had I done?

"Oh my God, get help!" I shouted. She suddenly looked so frail and afraid. She dropped the Gatorade, then dropped her phone as a nurse rushed out and wheeled her away.

Mail and newspapers were accumulating on the kitchen counter at the condo as her neighbors faithfully brought them inside each day. As I sifted through the junk mail, solicitations for charitable donations, and the Kohl's sales flyer, I spotted an envelope of the utmost importance— a bill from her insurance company. A quarterly payment was coming due for her long-term care insurance!

LONG. TERM. CARE. INSURANCE.

Finally, a bright spot in this horrible world of bundles, and tests, and broken windshields. Evidence of long-term care coverage meant she could stay in a nursing home or assisted living for a very long time— nearly eight years if we were doing the math correctly! I had visions of a large private room with mid-century modern furniture, perhaps traditional Lane end tables with matching lamps. There would be a glamour bath with all new towels, maybe some with embroidery and satin trim. I looked forward to going to Kohl's with her 30% off coupon and stocking up.

Finally, a plan was coming together! Maybe I'd pick up some skidproof bathroom rugs to match, and some nice crystal cut hangers to organize her new closet that we'd fill with pretty clothes, probably some new things by Vera Wang… they always fit her so well. I'd pick up her house plants from the condo, the African Violets that always bloomed right on schedule, and the Philodendron on the coffee table. I sure wish I would have inherited her green thumb! Also, I'd grab her New York Times crossword puzzle books, and a good CD player so her room would be flooded with the classics, just like our old house on Dorsetshire, where Saturdays were for brunch, Mozart, and sunshine pouring in the big living room window. We had plenty of time to figure all this out; we had eight years!

COVID-19 cases continued to climb, and guests were still prohibited in care facilities. My brother and I searched the internet and quickly agreed on a place that was everything a traditional nursing home was not. A video tour with the Marketing Manager showed a pristine facility, beautifully appointed with spacious apartments and an elegant dining room. Tables were set with fine china and cloth napkins; everything was sparkling clean. There were plenty of open areas to socialize, and garden, and read the daily paper. The website boasted a chef— a REAL CHEF— and a menu with plenty of nice choices, not the gross colorless slop that nursing homes usually serve. I imagined her appetite magically being restored, feeling relieved that she would soon be back to normal. Thank God this nightmare was almost over.

Though my intention was never to be a rulebreaker, I did want to spend a lot of time with my mom once she got settled. Cherry Tree Old Folks Home was a sprawling, ranch style compound near the outskirts of town, surrounded by meadows and countryside. The property backed up to a llama farm, owned by a retired dentist who sold Cherry Tree a parcel decades ago. Llamas are social animals. They not only need the companionship of other llamas, they love spending time with humans as well. The old folks at Cherry Tree were happy to comply, with snacks, snuggles, and weekly visits to the farm. The activities assistant loved animals, too. She was happiest when the residents were smiling.

That was before the global pandemic swept in, imposing a quarantine that stripped care facility residents everywhere of the few joys they had left. Even window visits were cancelled because staff were busy taking care of the residents who were sick with the virus. I could not imagine the trauma of dealing with critically ill old people all day. Would those sick with COVID-19 be sent to the hospital for care? Were ICU beds even available? Nursing homes initially had the highest exposure rate in the state. I wondered if my mom would be safe there. Either way, I was grateful there were people with the skills and dedication to help those folks who needed care the most. No one expected the staffing shortage that was about to unfold.

I had a recurring dream. I could hear my mother's voice on the phone. In barely a whisper she says, "Linda, I need your help… I really need your help." It's the reason I wanted to move her closer to me. After she was diagnosed, on our last phone call, I pleaded with her to move to Cherry Tree Old Folks Home. Initially she agreed and seemed excited about all that Cherry Tree had to offer. But now she was confused and forgetful, not even aware that we had had that discussion. My brother had already made a huge deposit to reserve a room and scheduled a mover. We were ready to go; however, she was not.

Diary of an Accidental Nursing Home Aide

"Mom, listen!" I shouted into the phone, thinking that the louder I spoke, the better she would understand me. "If you're at Cherry Tree Old Folks Home I can see you more often. You would like that, right? It would be just like when Papa was at the nursing home on Karl Road, and you stopped by every day after school to bring him a liverwurst sandwich and some German beer. You remember that, right?"

I should have given up and changed the conversation to something more benign, but I pressed on. "What if I could be there to see you every day? I could bring you snacks and show you dog pictures on my phone…"

She moaned, "COVID, no visitors."

"You let me figure that out, Mom. I'll come up with a plan and talk to you tomorrow."

Linda Lewis

Miss Yvette

"Do you have any skills? Have you worked at a nursing home before?" The lady on the phone at Cherry Tree Old Folks Home sounded distracted. She was having a snack, something crunchy.

"Well, not exactly," I replied, with a sugar-coated grin. "But I do have a magical umbrella that allows me to fly, and I can slide up a banister backwards! Does your building have a second floor?"

(Of course, I didn't really say that... although on my best days I can do both!)

What I actually said was, 'I'm very glad you asked! I was a hospice volunteer for many years. And I cherished my work providing care to the sick and dying. I have a whole stack of cards and letters from families who thanked me for spending time with their loved one."

"Right. When could you start?"

No training or credentials? Should I maybe take some classes? How could she possibly know I was a good fit for this position?

"If you can pass a criminal background check I can use you." Her name was Yvette; she sounded ambivalent and bored.

"Well, the last time I had a run in with the law, I was overparked in front of my daddy's nursing home in Cambridge so I could run him in a big ole jar of pretzels… you know, the ones they sell down at the Costco!" I had drifted into my southern accent without realizing it. The conversation made me uncomfortable.

Clearly not impressed, she said, "Cherry Tree Old Folks Home.com. Fill out the form; I'll call you." *Click.*

Here's a place that could use some kindness and good cheer, I said to myself as I hummed an old, familiar tune! *With every job that must be done there is an element of fun!"* They are going to LOVE having me on board.

Diary of an Accidental Nursing Home Aide

An in-person interview with Miss Yvette came one week later. I wore a fitted Dior skirt in crimson and wine, with a conservative blouse, my good pearls, and a Louis Vuitton Retiro, styled like Mary's trademark carpet bag. It was updated with traditional monogram canvas and red pebbled leather handles... just enough to show my fashion sense, yet not too flashy. My Louis Vuitton Stephan Sprouse or Murakami Cherry Cerise would have been overkill, and I wanted to make the right impression. I was certain Cherry Tree Old Folks Home did not want an employee who looked like a slob!

With both of us wearing masks, I stepped into Miss Yvette's cramped office. There were pictures of grown kids, little kids, old people and young people, some dressed up in their Sunday best for holidays and other special occasions. Beside a dusty desktop computer, I saw a stack of Styrofoam cups, a half-eaten Egg McMuffin, and a coffee mug that said *NO DRAMA LLAMA.* There was a vase with fake roses, a box of Anthony Thomas chocolates, and a Bible with a well-worn cover... keys, a bottle of hand lotion, and some wadded-up Kleenex on top of an application for a Travel Points Master Card. Post-it notes were stuck to every surface, the sign of a person who was probably doing the work of three. A glass jar of Skittles, stacks of papers, and a Bundt cake from a gas station mini-mart sat on a makeshift credenza. She looked overwhelmed.

I extended my hand and flashed a smile beneath my mask. "Miss Yvette, I have so looked forward to meeting you! How is your day going so far?" I took a seat in a folding chair beside the door and placed my bag discreetly at my feet. She looked at the LV, glanced at the rock on my hand, and grimaced. I met her gaze, smiled broadly, and said, "I know, right? I've been married two years, three years this April, and could not be happier! My husband is the most wonderful man... he is sooo good to me! I also have four little dogs, with another one on the way. I'll have to tell you the whole story sometime! Maybe we can go out to lunch!"

Miss Yvette reached for a chocolate and shoved it in her mouth, probably wondering why a rich white lady from the suburbs was applying for a job to change diapers and feed people at an old folks home. I sensed she was already betting against me.

"You may have noticed I completed all the online training and scored 100% on every module! I love learning new things! The video about handwashing and CDC infection control was outstanding! I'm all about preventing and containing the virus. We must pull together and do our part, right?

"You'll be working with Shanice and Patriciana. They will train you what to do."

Yvette's cell phone rang, and then her landline, and then a burner phone that she pulled from her bag. "No cell phones allowed on the floor. If I catch you I'll write you up." I stood up and did a little wave.

"It was wonderful to meet you, Miss Yvette. I can see you're busy; I can show myself out." Mary Poppins meets the Wicked Witch of the West. She silently hissed, "I'll get you, my pretty…"

While my plan to ambush Cherry Tree Old Folks Home with comfort and joy was unfolding nicely, things were not so good with my mom. I got a call late one night that she had been taken back to Cambridge Memorial Hospital with a temperature of 101. The aide on the phone said she might have aspirated some food, and also might have pneumonia.

High temperature and pneumonia? I knew there were active cases of COVID at her facility, but I had been assured earlier that day that my mom had tested negative.

The aide said she had been transported by EMS two hours earlier (and they were just getting around to calling me)? The girl on the phone sounded young and was clearly uneasy about our conversation. Perhaps my reputation preceded me. With my mother's diagnosis I knew it would eventually become harder for her to swallow. The part of the brain that controls that function was already compromised by the tumor. If she aspirated some food, that was probably the reason. I was not prepared to think about that yet.

Was she scared? Did she even understand why she was going to the hospital? It was the same place my dad went before he died. Was she thinking about that as the ambulance pulled up to the ER? Was she in pain? The aide reminded me that even if I did drive up there, I wouldn't be allowed in to see her because of COVID. Damn. The only thing that gave me hope was the time we would spend together at Cherry Tree Old Folks Home. She was treated at the hospital with antibiotics and released.

Diary of an Accidental Nursing Home Aide

Linda Lewis

Quite Atrocious

I arrived early for my first day of training as a nurse's aide with a notebook, a zipper bag filled with highlighters and pens, and a snack so I could study through lunch. I had not completed a CNA or STNA program, and I was eager to learn all I could about my new position. While I had no skills to speak of, I had been praying for an opportunity to be useful during the days of the virus and I was certain this was it. Miss Yvette told me they had their own training program, and judging by the company's marketing, everything that went on at Cherry Tree was best-in-class! A receptionist handed me a medical mask and took my temperature as a precaution, then keyed it into a tablet. It was one more way to guard against COVID-19 from entering the building. Next, I was introduced to a bearded fat man who was standing against the wall beside the ladies' room. He was wearing a janitor's shirt that barely buttoned across his considerable girth. I recognized him at once. His nametag said, Neil Lipman!

Neil Lipman was a former private eye who had been brought up on charges under the RICO statute for running stolen funds from Petoskey, Michigan to somewhere near Atlanta. He told the Feds he didn't know the money was dirty, and with no witnesses to testify against him, he got off with time served. His experience at Cherry Tree was not much greater than my own. "Small world," I sneered.

I followed my old nemesis through a glamorous lobby and a set of double doors, then past a dining room with beat up tables and broken-down chairs, nothing like I saw in the brochure pictures. We walked by some aides who were laughing and looking at their phones. "Hello," I said in a cheery voice! "I'm Linda, and I'm excited to be here! How is everyone today?" When we reached a metal door with no window, Neil tapped on the keypad. "2020 is the secret code. Can you remember that?" It was like choosing "password" for your password. Neil hadn't changed.

The dimly lit space beyond the door was a narrow hallway with stacks of boxes on one side, some stained upholstered chairs on the other, with tray tables arrange beside each one. There were boxes labeled *Creamed Corn*, and *Pineapple Chunks, no sugar added*. Another said *Super Clean Flushable Wipes*. Some of the boxes were dusty, as if they had been sitting there a long time. There was a toilet inside a crate, and some miniblinds still in the packages. Walkers and wheelchairs were pushed up against the wall awaiting repair. A mechanical lift had a post-it note attached that said, "Broken, do not use. See Neil." It was dated December 2019. This behind-the-scenes perspective painted a dismal picture, with floors that were grimy, and a mouse trap near the back exit. The space smelled sour and musty. "This is where you clock in... and this is where you'll take your break."

We continued down a main hallway past several patient rooms, and through a common area where people were gathered watching TV. "Hello, everyone! It's so nice to see you all! My name is Linda, and I look forward to hearing all your stories. We're going to have a lot of fun together!" I twirled my magic umbrella and waved, "Ta-ta!" Patriciana was waiting for me in a cramped office that smelled like every Bath and Body Works fragrance rolled into one. As a hospice volunteer we were taught never to wear perfume because some people are sensitive to strong smells. Certain fragrances can even trigger a headache. It was important to meet the needs of the person you were caring for; vanity was not part of the equation.

A tall garbage can was overflowing in the corner with used masks, gloves, and trash from McDonald's. On the desk there was a computer, a phone, and wire baskets full of gadgets— pagers, walkie talkies, pendants on strings, and a stack of tablets that looked like my iPad at home. There were other aides in the office who had just completed their shift. They were chatting away like old friends, but I didn't understand a word. I wondered if they also spoke English. Patriciana was sorting through a bin of pagers looking for one that worked. As she handed me the device, a muffled voice came over the walkie talkie.

"Shanice needs an assist in room 27," said Patriciana, translating the message to English.

"Me?" Wasn't there supposed to be some kind of training? How would I help Shanice if I didn't know what to do?

Already sweating under a mask, face shield, and a blue protective gown, I found the room, pulled on a pair of gloves, and let the fog on my glasses clear before I went

Linda Lewis

inside. "Knock knock," I exclaimed. "It's me Linda. I'm new here, but I'd be happy to help!" I walked in the room, noticed a horrible smell, and saw a man hanging naked from a hoist over the toilet. Something was dangling beneath him, almost touching the toilet seat. It was his scrotum. I gasped! Shanice explained he was struggling to have a bowel movement and had been hanging there for some time.

"Joo stay. I need wipes," she said, then disappeared. I waited with him, not sure if I was supposed to make small talk *(How 'bout those Buckeyes?)* or ask him to tell me a little bit about himself? Was he married, did he have kids? How did he end up here at Cherry Tree Old Folks Home? I stood outside the open bathroom door facing away from him and pulled the hem of my shirt up to my face trying to block out the smell.

My coworker returned; it seemed like hours. "Hold him steady; I will clean him."

Oh my goodness, oh my God, what have I gotten myself into? I held my breath, and when we were finished, ran to a nearby ladies' room and threw up.

I wondered if I had been the victim of some sort of cruel nursing home hazing ritual. Did Shanice stay away so long to see what I would do? To see if I would survive, or jump in my car and drive home like a fraidy cat who had seen a ghost— or worse!?

"Shanice," I whispered, when I bumped into her outside the restroom. "There is a huge box of wipes in the hallway by the time clock. Hundreds of packs! We could just grab a bunch and put a couple in every room! That way, when you need them, you don't have to leave the patient hanging while he waits. He didn't look very comfortable, and I'm sure he was embarrassed…"

"Joo. Need. The key."

"See, that's the thing… they're not even locked up, they're just sitting there! It looks like somebody opened the box already and took some."

Shanice walked me to the door next to the nurse's station and tapped her finger on the handle. "The key! The key!"

"Oh, okay… I understand." If the language barrier wasn't bad enough, the masks and face shields only made things worse. "Where can I find the key? Is there just one key and we all take turns? Do the nurses have the key? Shouldn't I have my own key in case I need supplies right away?"

She shrugged. Shanice was young, probably in her early thirties. She was obviously a nice girl with a big heart to do this type of work, and kind enough to take care of the man in the hoist without flinching. But she was assigned to teach me about my job, and we didn't even speak the same language. Surely, Miss Yvette would have considered this when she made the assignment...

Diary of an Accidental Nursing Home Aide

Lorna

Psalm 33:22 *Let thy mercy, O Lord, be upon us, according as we hope in thee.*

Before the week was over, I stockpiled the supplies I needed to be a nurse's aide at Cherry Tree Old Folks Home. When my coworkers were in the little office texting, I made my rounds, getting temperatures, chatting for a moment with the patients, and recording the data. But I was also keeping my eyes open, looking for opportunities to fill my secret supply closet. Housekeeping worked overnight. By morning they were tired, and not exactly vigilant about where they left their cart. The aides went through boxes of 30-gallon garbage bags, but if housekeeping forgot to restock, there were none. Dirty diapers piled up and the stench was blinding.

Diary of an Accidental Nursing Home Aide

I took some trash bags and then a few more. I stocked up on incontinence products, gloves, and bathroom wipes. The consequences of not having supplies immediately available for the residents meant needless delays in delivering care, and the discomfort of waiting to be clean. Hand soap, paper towels, and anti-bacterial products sat empty by the sink, so I started bringing my own. Though products from outside the facility were forbidden, I was willing to take my chances if it meant preventing the spread of germs during COVID. I was protecting my life as well. I also stocked up on fig-newtons, pudding cups, and juice boxes from the kitchen to help calm residents in memory care.

I complained to the administrant. I was outraged; my coworkers said nothing. I wondered if they were compliant because they needed the job, or if cultural differences prevented them from seeing the gravity of the situation. I had a week's inventory hidden in a kitchen cabinet above a centrally located refrigerator. There was so much emphasis on locking up the supplies, and time wasted chasing after the key. If Cherry Tree paid their employees a living wage, the workers might be less inclined to steal.

In the months I worked as an aide, I never had access to the supply closet, or authorization to get the products needed to prevent the spread of COVID-19. Even at the height of the pandemic, when stopping the virus in care facilities was paramount, supplies were lacking. While training videos on containing the spread were mandatory viewing, there was rarely a place to wash my hands with soap before putting on fresh gloves, or after taking a resident to the bathroom.

Further, there were residents who had no toilet paper, paper towels, or hygiene supplies in their bathrooms. Cherry Tree's leadership was weak, typically offering more excuses than results. While the administrant scurried about wiping down doorknobs, residents with no hand soap were spreading e-coli, touching everything in sight. My desire to stay with the patients through the worst days of the pandemic outweighed my desire to walk out. From the start, I knew my days at Cherry Tree were numbered. No one likes a precocious and persnickety lady from the suburbs who asks too many questions, and believes in hand washing after you poop.

How can this be? For residents in nursing homes who are on "the plan," the facility provides supplies for an exaggerated fee. They are charged for each diaper they use. One resident on the plan rejected a fresh pair of pull-ups at bedtime because the cost per pair was just too high. For the remaining patients, the adult children or spouse bring items as needed, including toothpaste, body lotion, deodorant, and shampoo. Since no visitors were allowed in the building, and many patients struggled to communicate their needs, no supplies arrived, and it was the residents who suffered.

One of my most cherished friends at Cherry Tree was a lady named Lorna. She was often confused and could no longer communicate. When I read to her from the Bible, however, she nodded and understood every word. Her relationship with her creator gave her peace. In Lorna's current state, she was unkempt, a little rough around the edges, and at times, difficult to manage. But when she leaned her head on my shoulder and I held her close, our friendship had depth beyond the words that were never spoken. We were sisters in Christ and valued that bond immensely. Lorna was defenseless, and I watched over her the same way I would have my own mother.

The aides had a nickname for her. When she shuffled out of her room in mismatched clothing, whether looking for companionship or something to eat, they circled around and clucked like chickens, eyes open wide, with an exaggerated grin. Lorna had the capacity to understand they were mocking her, but not the words to defend herself. Of the acts of abuse I witnessed as an aide, this was the most abhorrent. I should have reported it to the aide in charge, but she was the ringleader.

Nursing home aides, like all medical workers, are mandated reporters. They have regular contact with vulnerable people, and are legally required to submit a statement when abuse is observed or suspected. I took this mandate seriously. In my first week I filed three reports and quickly became the Cherry Tree pariah. Not only had I betrayed my coworkers, I gave them one more reason to see that I was different, an outsider who didn't know the system and would never fit in.

"Mandatory," I learned, was a term with a good bit of wiggle room. There was no reason to overreact to the things that went on with the residents. It was easier to simply look the other way than get involved. Aides did their work and went home. I went home wondering how I could fix a broken system, and thought about the people in my care. There was an aide who struggled with English and communicated mostly in her native Swahili. I knew she was withholding prescribed fluids from the residents at mealtime, which meant fewer glasses to wash, fewer diapers to change. Maybe she knew the consequences of dehydration, or perhaps not. Her training was likely no better than my own. I had to choose between the residents who needed to drink plenty of water, and a coworker who did not agree. She was outraged when I reported her, yet in the long run, I was the one who paid the price.

I was happy to help when a team lead assigned me to help with Lorna's shower. The residents were stinking of body odor and lack of personal care. There were remnants of food stuck to their faces and pajamas, while their hair was greasy and uncombed.

"She will go with you if you ask her. Lorna likes you," he said.

But Lorna didn't want to go. The community washroom was at the opposite end of the ward. I had never given anyone a shower, only because I had not been trained, and taking my chances on a slippery surface with an old, fragile person might have been disastrous.

"Hey, my friend." I wrapped my arm around her and gave her shoulder a squeeze. "I am so dirty and tired from working all day. As soon as I get home, I'm going to take a nice, hot shower." She tensed at the word. "I thought you might like to take a shower, too! It'll feel really good to get cleaned up, won't it?"

Lorna dug in her heels and shoved me away. My Mary Poppins powers of persuasion were not about to change the frightened woman's mind. So we took her by the arms, the team lead, a muscular Haitian man in his thirties on one side, and me holding the other. He was new. We walked; she sobbed. I assured her I would be with her the whole time. Lorna was stripped naked and placed in a plastic shower chair. The community shower had no doors or curtain. The team lead sprayed her down with water and asked me to hand him the soap and shampoo.

"There's no soap in the shower? There has to be soap in the shower!" I wondered if she was on "the plan."

"No soap," he confirmed.

"Umm, okay. Maybe there's some in the supply closet! Do you have the key?" The supply closet was on the other side of the building.

"What key?"

"The key for the supply closet. Everything is locked up here."

"Where do they keep the key? This woman is freezing!"

"You're the team lead... I thought you would have the key!"

"No... I know nothing about a key."

Diary of an Accidental Nursing Home Aide

I looked at Lorna, shivering and trying to cover herself. "Give me a second, I'll be right back!"

"What kind of place is this if there are no supplies for the residents? At my last job we had everything." He would figure that out soon enough.

Most of the residents were already asleep or watching TV. "Who's there? Who's there?" came a frail voice in the dark as I dashed into her room without knocking. I remained silent and tapped the flashlight app on my phone, then quickly sorted through her basket of personal hygiene supplies behind the toilet.

Another room, and another. Still no soap or shampoo! The temperature inside my protective gown and mask had gone up ten degrees and my eyes were burning with sweat. I thought of Lorna, agitated and confused, her long breasts hanging down over her belly, with an unfamiliar Black man looking on.

Linda Lewis

Flawed

Cherry Tree Old Folks Home is a place that exists nowhere and everywhere. It represents conditions at many facilities nationwide that put financial gain above all else. In my research, I discovered business models so convoluted and devious, that few outside the industry could tell who is taking out money, and where the profits are going. Corruption at every level is rampant. Award winning healthcare policy journalist Harris Meyer for AARP describes what nursing homes and long-term care facilities don't want you to know. (Italics are mine throughout.)

"It's tempting to heap blame on the owners of America's nursing homes," Meyer begins, "to argue that the pursuit of profits led to poor care and so many coronavirus-related deaths." He notes that while most care facility owners did their best to prevent the spread of COVID-19, it was the industry's "complex and murky financial structure that failed to safeguard the health of residents and staff." While few know just how much money long term care facilities bring in, COVID-19 has clearly hurt nursing homes financially.

"Fully 55 percent of them claim to be losing money, and 72 percent say they may not be able to sustain operations for another year, according to an August (2020) survey by the American Health Care Association and the National Center for Assisted Living. Even the nation's largest nursing home chain, Genesis HealthCare, says it's in jeopardy." Genesis has 360 facilities across the U.S. As of August the company was uncertain whether they would survive the coming year.

"Here is what you need to know to understand the business of nursing homes, and to what extent they caused the mess they are in." Meyer confirms my worst suspicion that long term care facilities are putting profits ahead of patient care. "Roughly 30 percent of nursing homes are owned by nonprofit organizations predominantly affiliated with religious groups, ethnic aid societies, and social service agencies. They strive to maximize revenue and efficiency, but any unspent funds are used to improve and expand their facilities. *The remaining 70 percent of homes are for-profit — free to pay out income to owners once they cover operating expenses and other obligations.* Owners include national chains, regional chains, and stand-alone facilities. About 1 in 7 for-profit homes are controlled by private equity investors."

Private equity facilities are on the rise in the U.S. The goal of the investors is to make the maximum amount of money in the shortest time possible by extracting profits from the companies they acquire. It has become an industry practice for these investors to cut corners at the expense of facility upkeep and resident care.

Meyer states that to understand nursing homes' finances, you have to start with their revenue. "Three-fifths of the nation's 1.3 million nursing home residents' fees are paid by Medicaid, the federal-state insurance program for low-income Americans. These older adults (and people with disabilities) often spend their remaining years in a nursing home, at taxpayers' expense. How profitable is the Medicaid business? It depends on who you ask. The average Medicaid payment, which varies by state, is around $200 per resident per day. But unlike a hotel charging that price, nursing homes have to provide hands-on care that many residents need with their daily activities. They also must provide meals, medical services and more. Nursing home operators consistently say that $200 doesn't cover their costs. Industry critics aren't so quick to agree, citing owners' opaque finances and multiple income sources. What is clear, is that the share of this revenue spent paying and training personnel (whether in government or private facilities) isn't enough. The industry's staff turnover is high, and there's a critical shortage of people qualified to provide patient care. This detracts from residents' well-being at any time, but it proved to be especially dangerous in 2020."

"Between May and October, the federal government pumped more than $21 billion into the industry in the form of grants, loans, and advance Medicare payments. Only $2.5 billion of that had usage stipulations; it's unknown how much of the aid went to stop the spread of COVID-19. 'Nursing homes can use it to shore up their bottom lines if they want to,' says Elaine Ryan, AARP's vice president of government affairs for state advocacy. 'We might never know where the money went.' A number of research studies have found that for-profit nursing homes generally have significantly lower staffing levels and quality of care than nonprofit facilities, as measured by the Nursing Home Compare quality star rating system run by the government's Centers for Medicare & Medicaid Services."

Here is why the rise of private equity care facilities is so damaging to an industry that is already struggling to maintain some level of respect. According to Meyer, "an estimated 10 percent of America's nursing homes are owned by private equity (PE) investment groups. Bankrolled by institutional investors and wealthy individuals, these firms typically buy businesses, make efficiency and/or cost-cutting changes to increase their apparent value, then sell them within three to five years. PE firms often borrow money against the businesses' assets and receive management fees as well as a share of profits when the enterprises are sold." Here is their usual practice as it pertains to nursing homes, according to Harvard University professor of health care policy David Grabowski and other researchers. "A firm will buy a nursing home, then place its buildings and other real estate — nursing homes' most valuable asset— in a separate holding company. Other companies also owned by the investors will start providing management, laundry supplies, and other services to the nursing home. These ownership structures make it hard to figure out who is responsible for the quality of care and how to recover damages if a resident is injured."

"Once a nursing home starts paying these related companies, says Grabowski, *the home may appear to be struggling, while at the same time the owners are making money from their other entities. The nursing home itself ends up saddled with debts incurred to pay off lenders who financed the PE firm's purchase."*

"The main reason these for-profit companies are in the nursing home business is to extract money through management contracts and lease agreements. They scream they have no money, but they've legally taken money out through all these related-party transactions. Deals like these," concludes Meyer, "have been going on for more than 20 years. Other for-profit firms have engaged in similar practices, separating out their real estate holdings and striking management and supply deals with related firms."

The article explains so much, but resolved so little for me, an accidental nursing home aide during COVID-19.

Diary of an Accidental Nursing Home Aide

Linda Lewis

Showtime

As COVID-19 spread, death rates among nursing home aides ranked among the highest of any job in America, according to the Bureau of Labor Statistics. What started as a desire to spend valuable time with my mom, put me on the front line of the pandemic, facing potential deadly consequences every time I showed up for work. I was stressed, but I knew God would protect me if I was there according to his will and purpose for my life; my heart was genuine. The workload was fierce, and the pressure to respond to call bells within the minimum time didn't go away because we were short staffed. Miss Yvette kept track on her computer to make sure the time limits and data sent to corporate didn't make her look bad, although I only saw her on the floor one time, pushing a resident in a wheelchair, and scolding me for not getting to the lady first. She was conspicuously absent as the rest of her team struggled.

The call pendants worn by patients at Cherry Tree are old. The strings are soiled and knotted, and the units themselves are faded to the shade of a vintage AT&T Model 100 Desktop phone. Most of the pendants page out correctly, but many cannot be cancelled once the resident's needs are met. Old alerts keep paging, again and again, three, four, five... a dozen times, long after the initial page is cancelled. I dreaded hearing Miss Yvette shouting into the walkie, "Somebody better cancel them penance! Room 29 is still waiting and corporate's gonna be mad."

I priced a new commercial pendant alert system and emailed the link to the administrant. Surely, he could understand the importance of replacing what was broken, especially when it impacts resident care. The product, installed, was so affordable I could have written a check to pay for it. Whether or not corporate was bleeding the facility dry, as Harris Meyer suggested, there wasn't a penny to be spared, and aides did twice the work necessary, running to cancel imaginary alerts while other patients waited. I hated inefficiency, but more than that, I despised neglect.

I started every shift overjoyed at the opportunity to serve. Within minutes, my face was dripping with sweat that pooled at the bottom of my mask, as did the snot from a chronically runny nose that couldn't be wiped. I couldn't see past the fog on my glasses, and wondered how many details I missed as a result. My hair stuck to the back of my neck, itchy and saturated, while drops of perspiration dripped down the inside of my polyester uniform. For eight hours I was soaked all the way through to my underwear.

The hourly pay rate was shameful for the amount of work the aides were doing. I made almost as much money babysitting in the seventies for three kids whose dad was the V.P. of Marketing for White Castle! I hated management's indifference as the workers suffered, both physically from the heat and exhaustion, and mentally for being dismissed as lower-class cheap labor. Unless I was on a boat on Little Traverse Bay, I preferred not to sweat. But now I was working for more than a paycheck. My life has been filled with adventure, prosperity, and blessings too numerous to count, and as cliché as it sounds, I wanted to give back. Despite management's deficiencies, Cherry Tree was where I wanted to be. But what about the residents? Should they be sacrificed on the altar of corporate greed, or as Meyer describes, a flawed business plan? I played along and flashed a big Mary Poppins smile as I breezed through the hallways, nodding dutifully at our leader's expressionless faces as they shuffled past. After all, the show must go on!

I had unwittingly joined the cast of a play, where we followed a script without questioning outcomes, and answered pendant calls with ambivalence. Room by room we completed tasks on people, ignoring their humanity while we sacrificed our own. There were characters, props, and a script, but no compassion. I was just another girl in the chorus with a walkie talkie, dancing around in my uniform with a big fake grin. "I'm here with your mid-afternoon snack, Mr. Jones. *Fa la, Fa la.* Would you like some vanilla wafers and a nice cup of juice? Maybe this afternoon we can build a marshmallow snowman together! Wouldn't that be fun?"

Whatever the leadership wasn't telling us, their cold, myopic dispositions were unsettling for workers at the bottom of the food chain. Among the leadership, few had college degrees or any training past high school. Each had been employed at Cherry Tree the same number of years, 17 to be exact. Their guarded nature created distrust, while the group's lack of credentials in health care baffled me. I secretly wondered if they were really humans, or robots taking orders from the Mother Ship.

"Well, good morning, Helga! How's your day going so far?" Helga was the office manager.

She looked as though she had just bitten into a bad shrimp.

Helga was exiting the supply closet empty handed, which made me wonder what she was doing in there, if not stealing wipes. It seemed we were heading in the same direction, so I tried again.

"I really like dogs... do you have any dogs at your house?"

No comment. Obviously, it was a difficult question.

"The first Ohio State game is Saturday. Do you like football? O-H, right?" Everyone likes the Buckeyes, surely she would say *something*.

She glanced my way, but her expression was vacant... apparently the only person in Ohio who didn't follow college sports. I had nothing to lose, so I tried one more time.

"I like those earrings, Helga. Are they David Yurman?" She stopped walking; we both stood silent. *Ha ha, just kidding.*

Diary of an Accidental Nursing Home Aide

Maybe their sour faces and flat personas were the result of being in the same job too long. Fortunately, I was just passing through, *Fa la, fa la.*

I wanted to get to know the people I was caring for, to listen to their stories, and give them a chance to be heard, perhaps for the last time. The loneliness and depression among the residents at Cherry Tree was palpable. While some could give words to their sadness, others were confused and felt abandoned. Spending time with the patients, however, was not in the script. I wondered… does a decorated U.S. Marine really want to do a craft with marshmallows and toothpicks? Does a retired Detroit cop really want a new coloring book? Respect does not ignore a lifetime of achievement by handing over a pack of crayons and a picture of the Easter Bunny. I wanted to know what they were proud of, their first car, a pretty girlfriend in high school, and the time their team won the city championship. They were still real people after all, with tales about siblings, and summer vacation, and the time they threw a football through the neighbor lady's front window.

Did Helga and the other robots know that even the hungriest resident would give up food for a week in exchange for a nice conversation? Why did they keep looking away when they could have made a difference? Even with the wrath of Miss Yvette shouting on the walkie, I would honor the residents in all the days that remained.

Diary of an Accidental Nursing Home Aide

Linda Lewis

Audrey

"Hello, hello!" I said with a smile! I adjusted my Mary Poppins hat and secured a daisy that had come loose on the brim. It was a tight fit over my face shield. "You must be Audrey!"

"Don't talk to her. She's non-verbal," barked a coworker passing by.

"Poppycock," I shouted back. "How will I know till I've tried?"

Audrey was in her room waiting to be taken to dinner. She looked like the cover of this month's Town and Country, dressed in Lilly Pulitzer and a floral scarf. The rooms in this part of the building were typically littered with used cups, yesterday's food, and pills that never got swallowed, but these residents rarely complained. Audrey's room, however, was a quiet cottage at the end of a garden path, a pot of gold beneath an imaginary rainbow. The quilt on her bed was alive with bold prints and delicate patterns, saturated in shades of springtime, and neatly stitched together like the years of a purposeful life. There were drapes in a coordinating shade, and throw pillows arranged with care. Every surface was dusted and clutter free. Her family was vigilant about her care, keeping close watch even during the pandemic. It made all the difference.

Her fine hair reached her shoulders. It was stylishly combed with a side part, and secured with a bobby pin. She had a sweet demeanor and perpetual grin— rare qualities for an old woman whose days were nearing the end.

I gave her hand a little squeeze, and discreetly snatched a framed photo from her nightstand as I wheeled her out to the dining room. Patients who are no longer able to feed themselves need extra time and care at mealtime. For some people it's difficult to chew and swallow; it's important to pay attention. As a hospice volunteer I was fortunate to have excellent training and mentorship. It was an intimate part of my job that I enjoyed.

Audrey studied me, watching my every move as I spooned small bites into her mouth. I talked about my dogs, my husband, and the places I'd travelled. I knew she wouldn't be offended. I could tell from her room that she had lived a privileged life, too. My coworkers were busy feeding residents, dropping food, and scrolling on their phones while their patients chewed. The coast was clear for me to go off script, and I put the framed photo on the table in front of her.

The picture was of a Chris Craft Constellation, the legendary "Chris Connie" motor yacht that was the darling of every marina in the 1970s. There were suntanned kids in swimsuits wrapped in towels on the aft deck, while the grownups, sipping cocktails, looked on. The image in the background was the Little Harbor Club on Little Traverse Bay, the crown jewel of Northern Michigan boating where I spent many summers.

"Audrey, this is such a beautiful picture! Is this your family?" I offered her another bite. While she chewed, I continued. "What beautiful children... it looks like three boys and a girl?" A sense of wonder washed over her; her eyes open wide. I leaned in closer. "Going by their ages, I bet they're all grown up by now... maybe they even have kids of their own..." I put my hand on her shoulder and smiled. "Audrey, do you have any grandchildren?" She beamed. We were making a connection.

A coworker brought around apple tarts for dessert. "I boated on Little Travers Bay for years," I went on. "We had a cottage on Bay Street and an old HackerCraft... a triple cockpit that we kept down at Walstroms." Her eyes were dancing; she stopped chewing. The team lead tapped her watch and scowled at me. I offered Audrey a sip of water holding a straw to her mouth.

"Do you remember where this picture was taken?" I looked in her eyes and waited. She was going back to that day, reliving that moment in the sunshine, searching for the words.

She was thirty years young again, smiling and bright. "Harbor Springs," she said. "It's Harbor Springs."

Linda Lewis

Du, du, liegst mir am Herzen

My phone rang. A nurse at the rehab suggested we start my mom on hospice. A social worker could complete the paperwork, and she could begin receiving palliative care that night. I understood that her condition was terminal, at least in an academic sense. But I couldn't grasp the thought of her not being here— for me, for my brothers, for the ladies who do scrapbooking on Monday nights. I reviewed, once again, the timeline of how quickly things had unfolded. She went to Cambridge Memorial in July, and rehab a few days later. It had only been four months since she got sick. What was I missing? I reviewed my notes, the bundle, the conversations I had with her doctors at the hospital. Desperate and afraid, I looked at the information from the neurological oncologist, and the notes I made during the conversation with the brain surgeon. Should we have done the biopsy? Can we still do it? Even though it would mean shaving her head and drilling a hole through the front of her skull, could it save her life? We could get a firm diagnosis— malignant or benign! What if it wasn't a glioma at all? Maybe she was an outlier and it was a different kind of tumor all together?

We authorized hospice care to begin. Visitation rules at nursing homes were different for patients who didn't have much time. I recalled the years— good years— I spent with terminally ill people in their final days. How a reckless socialite in her thirties ended up caring for the sick and dying is a powerful story, an unexpected answer to prayer and divine providence. I wrote about it in detail in my book, *Shoes for an Imaginary Life*, and treasure those moments and memories immensely.

Despite the erroneous belief that people in hospice care die sooner, or worse, that hospice causes death, waiting till the end only robs loved ones of far better care and pain management than they would receive otherwise. I once knew a World War II veteran with Alzheimer's whose terminal diagnosis lasted for two years, and his hospice care was renewed again and again. We played cards as he told me his stories. Sometimes he even let me win.

My phone rang again. With less than 24 hours in hospice, my mom was actively dying. The nurse said I should come. As I write, it's only March, four months after my mom left us. It seems like yesterday, and also a long time ago. I still think that if I send her a chapter to review, she will edit the pages with a red pen and mail them back to me with corrections.

I live across the street from the high school Tim and I attended forty years ago. When I turned sixteen she got a new VW Rabbit, and gave me her 1973 VW Super Beetle. The place where I write my stories faces a dining room window with a view of the school parking lot, the spot where she used to drop me off until I could drive myself.

Beyond the school I can see the old Northland Jaycee Pool, the sight of it, now in shambles, pushes me past the brink of nostalgia, wishing for just one more day we could spend there as a family. I re-watched the tapes in my head from the 1970's, and saw myself as a teenager in a white swimsuit, tan and already chasing boys, and my brothers doing cannon balls off the high dive. My mother, beautiful and young, watched over the top of her book and cheered them on. Whether it is cathartic to face the window and revisit those old times, I can't say. It doesn't feel right, nor does it feel entirely wrong. Tomorrow it will probably feel different.

It was a Friday. I gathered up some things I knew my mom would enjoy on our final earthly visit together. I opened the iTunes app and typed 'German Beer Drinking Songs' in the search box. I listened to a few and purchased the ones that were familiar. I searched for accordion music and Oktoberfest, and did the same. Some of the songs she sang to us as children did not appear to be available, so I brushed up on my German and decided I would sing them for her.

I found a picture book of our last visit to Harbor Springs, and an album we made for my parents' 40th wedding anniversary. There were photographs of the grandchildren, our dogs growing up, a trip to Saint Augustine, and all the things we did as a family when we were little. I shoved them in a Vera Bradley tote bag in 'Petal Paisley,' one of her favorite patterns. I threw in some Werther's Originals and Little Debbie Swiss Rolls, knowing full well that people don't eat when they're dying, but hopeful some snacks might change the outcome.

She was conscious but not really awake. She liked the German Beer Drinking songs and grinned; a flutter of her eyelids peeking out at me as if to say so. Other times I had visited she was wearing the new blue nightgown I got her, and seated in a wheelchair looking unkempt and disheveled. But now she was in a hospital bed, propped up with her head on two pillows, with her hair washed and neatly brushed. It was so long compared to how she always wore it. Starched white sheets were pulled up to her neck, folded over and smoothed straight across.

I had never touched my mother's hair. I played the accordion songs and stroked her gray locks the way I always had with my hospice patients. She smiled a tiny smile and hummed along. An aide peaked in, scowled, and gave me the signal to put on my mask. I ignored her. I knew the facility had active cases, but I got tested twice a week at work, for God's sake. I couldn't possibly have COVID-19. I was sobbing at my mother's bedside, wiping tears with my tee shirt, and people were still thinking about the damn virus! I couldn't save her. Of all the things I tried, there was nothing I could do. We looked through the scrapbook, me narrating the photos and trying to add a little humor. The corners of her mouth turned upward; I knew she was still there. Choking back tears, I started to sing the folk song she sang to us as children.

Du, du, liegst mir am Herzen,
Du, du, liegst mir im Sinn.
Du, du, machst mir viel Schmerzen,
Weißt nicht, wie gut ich dir bin.
Ja, ja, ja, ja, weißt nicht wie gut ich dir bin!

You, you are in my heart.

"My German is still really bad, isn't it, Mom." She nodded; her brow was furrowed in pain. It was selfish to hold off on her first dose of morphine, a family decision I did not agree with. I was too heartbroken to stay, yet I couldn't bear to leave her. She was resting now, no longer responsive. I took a stack of cards from her nightstand and opened each one. "Here's one from the so-and-sos on Dorsetshire, Mom. You remember when Tommy was best friends with Eric…" And then another. "How 'bout this beautiful card with all the flowers. It looks like everyone in the choir signed it." Dozens and dozens of cards, each lovingly narrated, knowing that the sense of hearing is the last to go.

"You were a wonderful mom," I leaned in and whispered. "I learned so much from you. Remember how you used to drive me to piano lessons every week at Mrs. Powell's house in Westerville? And how you taught everyone in my Girl Scout troop to sew an apron? I got a lot of badges because you helped me, Mom…" Badges for scouting, badges for life. So much of what she did for me as a girl is with me still, all these years later. I was a terrific writer even as a kid, because she made me read books and look up words in the dictionary. I still called her if I was knee deep in a manuscript struggling with subject verb agreement… or at least I did.

Until she got sick, every phone call began with, "Are you writing? What page are you on?" I never told her that I write my books from the inside out. It was better to simply ask if I could mail her a chapter. One of my favorite recent memories began with a visit to Oakland Greenhouse to buy geraniums. It's the day we took the picture on the cover. After she touched every plant and said hello to all the shoppers, she said we needed to make a few stops around the neighborhood before I took her home.

I knew she was selling copies of my first book to everyone in sight! Maybe I don't remember the times she was proud of me growing up. Maybe I was rebellious and didn't care. But boy was she proud of me now… her daughter the writer who writes real books and here is a copy I can sell you! My books opened up a whole new world for us, a mother-daughter team where I wrote the stories and she promoted them. I'm so glad we did that while there was time…

"Now, just pull into the driveway on the left, after the big rock. My friend, Alice, wants you to sign her book."

Good lord…

Book in hand, Alice came bouncing down the porch steps with her copy of *Seeking Miranda*. I twisted my face into a smile… oh my gosh, this was so painfully awkward! My mom waited in the car while I penned the inscription. *"For Alice, All My Best… Linda Lewis.* Date, smiley face, underlined, done. Alice's husband took pictures. We made five stops in all; my mom was beaming.

"You did a great job raising us three kids, Mom… We're going to be okay you know." I was sobbing openly; a difficult and awkward moment since Germans are rumored never to show emotion. The box of Kleenex on the nightstand was empty so I blew my nose on my sleeve.

Diary of an Accidental Nursing Home Aide

"I know you worry about Tommy. Remember when we lived in New Hampshire and he was around three years old, and he snuck outside with the dog and we found him in a snowdrift?" No response, but that was okay. There was no doubt she was thinking of him, wondering if her prodigal son would come home to say goodbye. Tommy was the middle child— living out of state, troubled, and in poor health. With no known address and no money, he had no idea how much his mother needed him.

Only one person was allowed in the room at a time. My other brother was in the lobby, waiting his turn. A successful businessman, his time was valuable. I kissed my mother's forehead and said goodbye. It was life and death in the days of COVID.

I crawled into bed early with a migraine, feeling weak and dehydrated from crying so many tears. Tim and the dogs were waiting for me. I ate two packs of Little Debbies from my tote bag and felt worse. Already snuggled under the covers, our yorkie, Simon, bounded out and snatched the cellophane wrapper from my hand, then dashed under the bed to swallow it. Tim grabbed a handful of Cheerios from a sealed canister that we keep on the dresser for situations like this. He tossed them into the hallway to distract the dogs, while I reached under the bed to remove the contraband. Similar antics would repeat themselves that night, but I enjoyed the chaos; it was a happy distraction. I recalled that my mom used to pray for Simon, knowing how he struggled to be a better boy. I smiled.

My phone rang. I could see from the caller ID it was my brother conferencing me in with a call from the rehab. "I have the hospice nurse on the other line. Can everyone hear me?" I wasn't expecting this call.

"I'm here with your mother," the nurse said quietly.

"Hello," I tried to say but no sound came out.

"Your mother's heartrate has slowed to blah, blah, and her blood pressure has dropped to blah blah, over blah."

"I'm getting in my car and coming up there," I jumped out of bed, ran downstairs, and grabbed my keys, not concerned that it was November and I was still in my nightgown.

"Wait," said my brother who apparently had information I did not.

"It's too late," said the hospice nurse whose name I never even heard. "Her respirations are faint, and far apart. I'm sorry."

Instead of being surrounded by her loved ones, a stranger was narrating her final moments, a conversation our mother could hear as well. It was uncivilized; it was obscene. This was no way to die, but it was life and death during the days of COVID. I wanted to scream STOP, but instead I waited in stunned silence listening on speaker phone. I hated the virus, and I hated the nurse for taking my place at my mother's bedside.

"I don't hear any more respirations… I think she's… no, wait, wait… there, she just took a small breath. Let's just wait another minute… no, I'm sorry, I'm afraid she's… No, there's another breath, she's a fighter… I'm sorry it has to be this way, but with COVID-19 and all, well, you understand." My mom took her last breath and she was gone. A stranger held my mom's hand as she died, and no, I didn't understand.

Linda Lewis

Catching COVID

Five days later I was diagnosed with the virus. I had been sleeping a lot, feeling miserable, and justifiably so. I hadn't even begun to grieve my mother's passing, and now I had COVID-19. I wasn't eating enough, and I was watching too much TV. There were stories of politicians stomping their feet over the election results, and reports of white cops killing Black men all over America. The number of people who had died from the virus was climbing, while others refused to acknowledge that the pandemic existed at all. Testing at work was supposed to protect the staff and residents. I wished I would have better protected myself as well.

I was symptomatic, but not as sick as a lot of people. My doctor prescribed prednisone for systemic inflammation, plus Tylenol and bedrest. I was quarantined

Linda Lewis

14 days and stayed in the guest room until the symptoms passed. I missed my mother's funeral. Isolation was a grievous assault on the hearts and sensibilities of families everywhere, but especially my own.

In the weeks I was absent, the number of patients in quarantine at Cherry Tree Old Folks Home was rising, and coworkers stopped reporting for work. Some were sick with the virus themselves or caring for family members who were ill. Schools were closed and children couldn't be left home alone. Our workforce was dwindling, and shifts were frequently short one or two people. At the time, I could not imagine how things could get much worse.

Whether due to HIPAA regulations or fear that aides could not be trusted with the information, it was never clear which patients were sick. One day I was taking a man to the bathroom and helping him into bed. The next day I learned he died hours later from COVID. Did the leaders think the aides were too backward and ignorant to understand? Or were we replaceable, our lives not worth protecting?

There were whispers of who had the virus and who was in isolation due to possible exposure. If a resident left the building, whether for an hour or a weeklong hospital stay, all were confined to their rooms upon return. Isolation notices were taped to their doors. Staff ignored the warnings and cared for residents in the usual way, often without protection. Sometimes the signs were taken down by residents who didn't understand the gravity of the situation, proving the system ineffective. Everyone in the building was required to wear a mask, but people in memory care often forgot. Patients wondered out of their rooms and into the hallways, even passing through security doors that were armed but broken. With so few staff on board, it was impossible to watch everybody at once.

A lady in memory care shuffled out to the common living room with her pants down around her ankles, her mask beneath her chin.

"I'm all out of toilet paper," she announced. "And I need some now... RIGHT NOW!" Of course, I didn't have a key to the supply closet, and my personal inventory, though well stocked, was two wards away. I would never make it there and back in time. I dashed into a nearby kitchen for some paper towels; naturally, the holder was empty.

It wasn't just that she squatted and pooped in the living room while other residents looked on. The humiliation and neglect that patients were forced to endure was appalling. Was it worth keeping vital supplies under lock and key if this was the outcome? Was the operating budget so meager that toilet paper had become a luxury, or was there more to it than that?

When I spoke with the marketing director at Cherry Tree Old Folks Home about admitting my mom, she stated that privately owned (for profit) care centers were able to provide *more services and better care* because they had the flexibility and resources that government/Medicaid homes did not. She said the ratio of staff to residents at Cherry Tree was higher, when in fact, the opposite was true. Currently, there is no set rule for staffing a facility compared to its census data. As a result, residents of for-profit facilities are nearly twice as likely to suffer from health issues as a result of poor care. Further, nearly 75% of nursing homes operate on related party transactions, a business practice where the owners outsource certain aspects of care to companies they also control. This allows the owners to pay themselves using the nursing home's budget, and explains why there is no toilet paper for the lady in memory care.

Diary of an Accidental Nursing Home Aide

Linda Lewis

My White Privilege

Tim and I grew up blocks apart in an exclusive Columbus suburb, with brand new schools, the best teachers, and every activity you can think of. Girls took ballet and piano lessons; boys played in traveling soccer leagues. The marching band had expensive uniforms, and our parents went to all the games; in our neighborhood, mothers didn't work. We had ten-speed bikes, and motor homes, and boats to go waterskiing. We took vacations to Disney World, and class trips to Cedar Point. Season passes to the Northland Jaycee Pool were a luxury taken for granted, and there was no limit to how much candy we could afford to buy at the snack bar. Life was a bottomless pit of treasures and games that were ours for the taking. There was little concern for the families beyond our tidy, perfect streets. I wasn't even allowed to ride my bike across Morse Road. How could I possibly know what was out there?

Tim left Columbus for a career in the music industry. As an audio engineer, he hit the road with a long list of rock bands, managing tours, and doing shows with stars everyone's heard of. (Reba McEntire was a pleasure to work with, Streisand not so much.) From large venues to festivals and county fairs, he was surrounded by people from all walks of life. His lightheartedness and talent for delivering a punchline made him welcome wherever he travelled. He was sophisticated yet approachable; he understood the ways of the world.

I left Columbus after graduating from Ohio State and married a well-to-do dentist with a growing practice and his eye on a prosperous future. Not unlike my growing up years, I had a cleaning lady, a credit card, and a man to take care of the lawn. I had little responsibility beyond making charming small talk at dinner parties and always looking my best. The Black families lived in one part of town, the whites in another. There were suburbs with higher taxes and the best schools. Houses in those areas were the most expensive, and only people with high paying jobs could afford to live there. It was normal because *it had always been normal.*

I had a degree in education and did substitute teaching in the city schools. I met a third grader whose parents were both in prison. At eight years old his teeth were completely rotted. In another part of town there was a ten-year-old who spoke as if he had been watching porn all night instead of doing his homework. At a different school, there was a little girl in braids who snuck up behind me on a snowy day. It was recess and we were freezing! She slipped her hands into the pockets of my goose down coat (new that season from Lazarus), and said, "You know what I like about you, Miss Linda? I like you because you is always so warm." I noticed the girl was not wearing any gloves.

I addressed the issue of my white privilege (though nobody actually called it that), by purchasing brand new coats, hats, and mittens for every kid in her class. I had no idea the crisis was so deep rooted and woven into the mix of society. In my ignorance, I thought I was a problem solver, a hero.

My white privilege continued into my thirties with well-to-do neighbors, and proper friends at the yacht club where we kept our boat. We golfed and went swimming at the country club, and attended important society affairs like symphony concerts and the Fine Arts Ball. While kids in the Black neighborhoods couldn't afford shoes, I had dresses that cost as much as someone's car. Even with homes in three states, the only Black people I knew about were the ones on TV, and the pool man. It was not until decades later that it occurred to me: Perhaps while I was enjoying my good life, there were folks in other places who would enjoy the good life, too.

Linda Lewis

Racial and Ethnic Disparity in the Workforce.

When it comes to racial disparity among the long-term care workforce (of which I was now a part), Black employees and immigrants make up more than half of direct care workers, a group which is often marginalized and overlooked. They are employed in nursing homes, assisted livings, long term care facilities, private homes, and hospitals. The position specifically involves helping people with activities of daily living, or ADLs. This includes feeding, bathing, transferring, toileting, dressing, and continence care, (which means cleaning and diapering people after they go to the bathroom).

Linda Lewis

Leah Zallman is Director of Research at the Institute for Community Health and Assistant Professor of Medicine at Harvard Medical School. In her research she found that "50% of all Black/African American aides have a high school education or less. Immigrants are the most formally educated of the group, with 62% having some college or higher. Whites in these roles have the least amount of education and an average older age than the other groups. Once a worker is stuck in this role, it's hard to move up or move out."

At Cherry Tree Old Folks Home, I was paid $12.50 an hour, which is slightly less than the statewide average. Aides with credentials like STNA or CNA make a little more. With income well below the poverty level, it is hard to expect workers to care for your family members when they're not paid enough to provide for their own. Many direct care workers maintain two full time jobs to make ends meet. During COVID, this meant twice the exposure and increased risk of spreading the virus to residents and staff. At Cherry Tree the practice continued uninterrupted, while management looked the other way.

Care aides who work only one full time job often rely on public assistance to get by. According to Steven Campbell, Data and Policy Analyst at the Paraprofessional

Diary of an Accidental Nursing Home Aide

Health Institute, "improving the income and lives of these workers would increase the quality and stability of care for the nation's seniors proportionally. If the senior population doubles by 2050 as expected, where will we find the workers to take care of them when nursing home aides are already in short supply? And who will choose this role over less demanding alternatives if compensation does not improve?" In the time of COVID, care facilities saw an exodus of workers who went to work at warehouses, factories, and fast-food chains to make more money and reduce their risk of getting sick. Whether they return to their jobs as nurse's aides to do more work for less money remains to be seen.

Employee retention at care facilities was at crisis levels long before the start of the pandemic. Whether employees were fired (like me), or they simply moved on to what looked like greener pastures I'll never know. There were so many secrets. Aides from local staffing agencies were available to cover shifts, but at twice the price. When I asked Miss Yvette why we couldn't hire help to get us through the crisis, she only replied, "Because we're not doing that, that's why." There were mysterious dismissals, suspensions, and people on administrative leave. Some of the aides got tired of doing the work of three and walked off the job. Yet, the leaders remained dismissive and aloof. Were they fully human, or badly programmed Borg drones from the Starship Voyager? I shuddered when I heard a voice say, *resistance is futile...*

I learned about our first resident with COVID-19 by reading his obituary on Facebook. A week earlier, there was a fire drill, and following protocol, I hurried to that section of the building to help move residents to safety. The alarm was painfully loud, as fire alarms must be. Patients were frantic, and holding onto one another for emotional support. I arrived at the alarm's source to find that Neil Lipman intentionally set a small fire to test the system without first warning the staff. The patient with COVID was housed in that part of the building, steps from the hallway where the employees were gathered waiting for the 'all clear.' The man died at the hospital days later. The leaders knew he had the virus; the aides who took care of him did not.

My coworkers were ambivalent, but I was outraged. I wondered again whether their acceptance of the deficiencies at work were tied to their upbringing and mores at home. Maybe the conditions where they grew up were so much worse that they thought Cherry Tree was adequate, possibly even exceptional by comparison. Or perhaps they were glad to simply have a job, *any job* where their heavy accents and lack of cultural awareness would provide some income to help their families. Many were saving money to sponsor relatives in their journey to America, while others were paying for school. Their work ethic deserved far more than what they were getting, and that included protection from a virus that could kill us all.

Far too many things were out of order. I made a list, certain the administrant would appreciate my interest in bringing Cherry Tree up to my acceptable standards.

"In every job that must be done, there is an element of fun," I said to the administrant as I handed him my clipboard. *"You find the fun and snap! The job's a game!"*

"I don't work on the medical side," he said without looking up from his phone.

I wanted to say, *Dude... everything in here is the medical side, because everyone here is old and sick!* But instead, I said, 'I bet we could knock out that list in no time if we all worked together! Maybe we could even order pizza! It would be fun, right?" I saw a robin fly by, whistling a happy tune, and then another...

"That's the medical side, the medical side. Nooo, I don't work on the medical side."

Linda Lewis

Putzfimmel... the German Way

There was a right way and a wrong way to do everything, as every German mother knows. But where did our busy mom find the energy to keep everything clean and in perfect order while never looking away from the children in her charge? Half the kids on our street stopped by in the morning for a Pop-Tart on the way to the bus stop, and again for cookies and tea on the way home. Our mom was always prepared.

The house on Dorsetshire was the place where all the good birthday parties happened, and all the best sleep-overs, too! Yet, despite the busy schedules of three children, our house was on a revolving schedule of cleaning and tidying that surpassed the most fastidious housekeeping rules of the day. All the Hummel figures were lovingly dusted every week, not by moving things willy-nilly around the end tables (the way I do it), but by carefully removing each item— the figurines, the vase, the Mid-century ashtray. Each piece was placed on the good sofa, and polished with a soft cloth (not a Swiffer with a plastic handle). My favorite Hummels were *Goose Girl* and *Stormy Weather*, the same ones that sit on our end tables today, lovingly dusted.

After dusting, and *only* after dusting, linoleum floors were made spotless on hands and knees with a scrub bucket and rag. It was backbreaking work, but that was the German way. Carpeted floors were vacuumed by an Electrolux canister sweeper, leaving tracks that were too straight to step on. Area rugs were taken outside and shaken by hand, a task that I still do today, an old German woman of 58, just like my mom.

Sheets and towels were laundered every Wednesday with extra detergent and hot water, then folded correctly—the long way, then in half, and in half again. *You wouldn't want to dry a clean body with a dirty towel, now, would you?* Folding sheets was a two-person job if it was to be done the right way. With me being the oldest, and Tommy being too sloppy, I was always the one to help. We stretched out the sheet, pulling it taught between us, folding it corner-to-corner once, then corner-to-corner again. My little brothers ran beneath it screaming like Indians as we smoothed the seams and walked the ends toward each other, my mom and me, leaving the finished product so tightly folded it could fit back in the package it came in.

In the kitchen, pots and pans were nested one inside the other, with the lids stacked beside them. Glasses were neatly staged on cabinets lined with shelf paper, and spices were displayed in a special rack, alphabetically arranged with labels facing forward. Dirty dishes went straight into the dishwasher, not the sink, and the microwave was wiped clean after each use. Burner drip pans were always shiny, never black from burns and spills. That was the German way. And if you think that's excessive, you should have met my grandmother!

Linda Lewis

Jack

Faith was a girl in her late twenties who left Nigeria for an education in the U.S. She was working at two nursing homes and studying to be a pharmacist. In her home country she cared for her grandparents and aging people in her community. No one was put in a facility to die; the generations looked after each other. She was smart and happy to share her experience, which, in the absence of formal training, was invaluable to me.

Faith was loud. Like all the aides from her part of the world, her broken English crackled through the walkie with the intensity of a police radio, and was every bit as alarming. She had a terrific sense of humor and teased me about our communication gap. I asked her to teach me something in her language, Hausa, so I could shout at her over the walkie talkie to get even. On a paper towel from my secret inventory, she wrote, *Ka sanya mai kyau aiki na shi.* I practiced it over and over, then finally shouted it with glee over the walkie, a smile in my voice. It meant, *You have made a good job of it.* Faith roared. My Hausa was even worse than my German! Miss Yvette said I needed to be more respectful of my coworkers or she would write me up.

There was a resident who collected vintage cars. The walls of his room were covered with photographs of the vehicles he owned through the years, and ads from Ford Motor Company picturing the same. By providence or by fate, I was a car fanatic too, and jumped at the chance to hear his story. When people are sick and dying, they often have a longing to talk about their past, their journey. It helps validate the time they spent on this earth, and also confirms that their memories have been embraced by someone who cares. Long term senior facilities are so understaffed and employees are so rushed, that emotional and spiritual needs are neglected or ignored completely. Listening was a gift I longed to share with everyone, one that would eventually lead to my dismissal.

Jack was a fan of fine automobiles from a young age, and took a job as a car salesman straight out of high school.

Diary of an Accidental Nursing Home Aide

His product knowledge was immense; his enthusiasm unstoppable, and the Ford dealership where he worked knew he was destined to be a star. When the other salesmen met for lunch at a nearby bar and grill, Jack grabbed a set of keys from the hook in the sales office and headed for the steel mill nearby. It was the mid 1960's. The New Boston Coke Corporation was in its heyday and employed nearly every able-bodied worker in town. The discovery of iron ore in the foothills of southern Ohio, along with its proximity to virgin forest tracts and two major rivers, made it the perfect site for blast furnaces and the mining of valuable resources. Jack grew up in the mill's namesake, Ironton. His first car was a 1965 Mustang that started as his demo, and was purchased when he had earned enough money.

"You've heard of Mustang Sally," he said with a grin. "Well, I called my '65, *Old Susie...* and boy, was she a beauty..." It was the nickname workers called the biggest furnace at the mill.

The men at New Boston had money to burn. They worked long hours, went home filthy and exhausted, then showered, hit the sheets early, and started all over again the next day. But one thing they always made time for was Jack, and whatever flashy car he pulled up in at lunchtime.

Jack parked in the grassy knoll across from the main lot. He brought coffee and donuts from the bakery across from the post office, and set up a card table he bought at a yard sale. Of the 4800 men employed at the mill, nobody knows exactly how many of them bought a car from Jack over his twenty-five years in the business, but legend has it that Jack sold something to damn near everyone.

As we chatted, I made his bed, picked up his room, and put his breakfast dishes on a tray to take back to the kitchen. I was already with him far too long but wanted to hear what happened next with the men at New Boston. I sensed Miss Yvette was watching me.

"Hold that thought, my friend. I want to hear the rest of the story." I dashed from his room to answer another call.

I stopped in the kitchen to grab a drink. It was critical to stay hydrated, especially while sweating continuously in full PPE. The dishwasher in that unit was ancient, and every clean glass that came out of it smelled like chicken broth, as did the water I drank. It was sickening but temporary, and I made a mental note to request a repair. The washing machine in that section didn't work, either. The plastic jug that hung on the wall wasn't releasing detergent down the hose and into the machine the way it should. The residents' laundry was not getting clean!! Much of it was soiled with urine, feces, and blood, and rather than fix the problem, we were drying and folding clothes that were carrying bacteria and stunk horribly. It was worse than the mess in the sink.

There were cabinet doors swinging off their hinges and into a common area. A woman diagnosed with dementia took me by the arm and said, "You know, if someone doesn't repair those cabinets somebody could hit their head and get hurt." That a resident with Alzheimer's had observed what management apparently had not, puzzled me. At a price tag of more than $5000 a month, there must be something left over for repairs. On Dorsetshire, we had a man named Mr. Thatcher, who lived one street over. He had a repair business that was supported by every lady in the neighborhood. No one on our street went more than a day with a broken appliance. How expensive could a new dishwasher be? We had over 100 residents and could not afford any downtime. (It wasn't until I left my job that I looked into the details and learned where the money was going.) The aides were encouraged to enter work orders for repairs on the tablet, but when I mentioned it, Patriciana scoffed.

"Do not waste your time, Miss Linda. They will do nothing." Before she hurried off to answer a call, she asked if I had a key to the supply closet. A resident needed toilet paper in a hurry.

There was a garbage disposal that didn't work, and a murky stew of gray water and mechanically ground food bubbled up in the sink after every meal, nearly reaching the top. The other girls reached through the slop with their hands to remove the clog.

"No, no!" I shouted. "This is disgusting! Let's fill out a work order and make them fix it!" My white privilege was bursting at the seams! "We could boycott and not do any work until they listened to what we have to say! C'mon, you guys… let's do this!"

Shanice giggled. "They will do nothing."

Like many workers in the long-term care industry, whether Black or white, I was a nameless, disposable worker, no longer a lady of means who was accustomed to being heard. I hated that we— all of us— were treated with disrespect and dismissed when we had a legitimate complaint. I was a troublemaker, an accidental nurse's aide who asked too many questions, and expected a straight answer.

Diary of an Accidental Nursing Home Aide

I wondered why my coworkers were not uphauled by these conditions. I regret not learning more about them, their lives in Africa, and their new lives here. I wish I could have heard their stories! I filled out the work order anyway. Every neighborhood has its own Mr. Thatcher, but I'm not sure that mattered. I continued to wonder about the corporate shareholders, the faceless men in suits, far away from the old people who mattered so little.

I clocked out for my break and headed for Jack's room. He was finishing his lunch. "I kept *Old Susie* till Nancy and I started a family." We picked up the conversation right where we left off. "I thought we all fit in the Mustang just fine, but Nancy wanted a station wagon."

I glanced at the picture on his nightstand. She looked like Grace Kelly. I was certain she got her way.

"As much as it broke my heart, I traded her in (the car, not my wife) on a 1972 Ford Country Squire, brown and tan with the wood paneling."

"Oh my God, Jack… that is the ugliest car ever made! How could you?!"

"Go ahead and laugh…"

"We had one at our house, too," I said, "a 1973. My dad travelled for work and flew out of Newark every week. It had a fold down seat in the back; I remember it well!"

"Whatever happened to it? Did he trade it for something more respectable?"

"No," I said, trying to get a discrete look at my watch to check the time. "We only had it for a month and it got stolen at the Newark Airport."

"Thank goodness for that! You must have been relieved..."

I laughed out loud! "Yeah, but only for a minute. The insurance paid for the car and we got another one just like it." I feigned trauma and upset for effect. "I struggled through most of my childhood, Jack. It wasn't easy." He was wiping tears from his eyes, laughing the big hearty laugh of an old, happy man. "What about your '72?"

"Well, not every family had two cars in those days, so I ended up driving the wagon, too. For about a week!" He roared! "I hated that car! Sold a bunch of 'em, never wanted to own one!" I was laughing too, now. A family photo with the old wagon hung in a frame by the window, Nancy and three small children posed beside it. He may have hated the car, but the picture was priceless.

Diary of an Accidental Nursing Home Aide

Jack needed to use the restroom. He was too heavy for me to lift, and Faith was already helping another resident. We were short staffed as usual, with two people doing the job of four, which used to be the job of eight. Many of the residents, like Jack, had put on weight due to inactivity during COVID-19, and their muscles quickly atrophied. Residents who used to be active sat quarantined in their rooms watching TV all day; many would never walk independently again. Now confined to a recliner or his wheelchair, I couldn't lift him.

I went to Miss Yvette for help. "Jack has put on so much weight and he's lost a lot of his strength. I need someone to help me lift him."

"What is your question." Her lack of enthusiasm exhausted me.

"He can't push off with his feet anymore when I try to move him."

"Hmm mmm," she replied.

"Maybe he could get changed from a one person assist to a two person."

"Make him pivot."

"He can't pivot."

"Yes he can."

"No, he can't! He's trying really hard but he just can't!"

"Sure he can. Tell him to pivot. Make him do it."

"He's not strong enough, he can't push off with his feet." That was the rule for a one person assist. If they can support at least some of their own weight, they can essentially help the aide move them. If they cannot support any weight, a person becomes dead weight. Jack's chart stated he weighed 250 pounds, but that was months ago. He was bigger than that now! I couldn't lift him no matter how hard I tried. When he needed to use the bathroom he would need more help than I could provide."

"He's manipulating you," exclaimed Miss Yvette. "I think he just likes the attention. You waste too much time talkin' to him. From now on, you just tell him you're busy."

"But he's still too heavy to lift. I can't lift him."

"He's a one person. You were trained. You can lift him!"

Months earlier, when I thought my mom would be moving to Cherry Tree, I read the admission contract, paid the deposit, and completed the application. It states that every resident's care needs were determined by regular assessments conducted by facility personnel. It gave me peace knowing that her care would increase as her condition declined. I believed the administrant and his team would provide what the contract promised.

Since 2013, a group of law firms has systematically sued several major nursing home chains, operating in California and throughout the U.S. New York Times journalist, Paula Span, explains.

"The letter went out to about 1,900 Californians from law firms bringing a class-action suit against one of the country's largest assisted-living chains. If the recipients, or their family members, had lived in a community operated by [one of those facilities] in recent years, 'we would like to speak with you regarding your residency and experience,' the letter said."

"It all boils down to the use of assessments, or lack thereof," said Kathryn Stebner, the trial counsel in the case. "These are à la carte facilities — the more needs you have, the more you have to pay. So, they assess you."

A lawsuit is now before the U.S. District Court for Central California. Charges were initially filed in 2017; the case is ongoing. The plaintiffs argue "that when staff members conduct such periodic assessments — to determine whether a resident needs help bathing or dressing, for example, or suffers from dementia — the facilities don't use the results to determine an adequate number of staff members," stated Span, in an article dated February 14, 2020, one month before COVID-19 unofficially began.

I was not surprised to learn that the complaint alleges that even when assessments are performed as promised by the admission contract, the care provided is based on pre-determined budget decisions and shareholder profits, while related staffing decisions are frequently ignored. "People pay more, but they're not getting more care," Stebner continued. I finally understood why Jack would never be a two person assist no matter how much weight he had gained. Like Harris Meyer, Kathryn Stebner agrees [the chain] is misrepresenting its practices and deceiving customers in violation of state business statutes, and lacks enough trained staff members to deliver the care specified in resident contracts and marketing materials... The business model is fraudulent, and it's putting people at risk," Ms. Stebner concluded.

The company, with more than 250 facilities nationwide, calls the charges "copycat allegations," based on similar tactics used against other long term care operations. They state the charges against them are baseless, and categorically false.

"Jack is a two person assist," I repeated to Miss Yvette, knowing my words had fallen on deaf ears. It was just another stop along my journey, a page in the diary of an accidental nursing home aide. There was so much fraud, so much misinformation. I had unintentionally become an advocate for the residents, and also, every administrant's worst nightmare.

Linda Lewis

The Five Star Myth

To help consumers sort out the good facilities from the bad, The Centers for Medicare and Medicaid Services (CMS) in January 2021 replaced their former rating system with a new program called *Care Compare*, that makes it easier to locate the best overall facility. The new plan simplifies the process by distilling volumes of information into a manageable product that is based on metrics, not emotion. Designed to educate consumers and attract new residents, the five-star rating scale became the primary measure of quality once the pandemic began, along with an alluring sales pitch by friendly marketing managers who get paid to keep their facilities full. Here's what you need to know:

Linda Lewis

Twelve years ago, The Centers for Medicare & Medicaid Services (CMS) enhanced its Nursing Home Compare1 public reporting site to include a set of quality ratings for each nursing home that participates in Medicare or Medicaid. The ratings take the form of several "star" ratings for each nursing home. The primary goal of this rating system is to provide residents and their families with an easy way to assessment of nursing home quality, making meaningful distinctions between high and low performing nursing homes. This document provides a comprehensive description of the design for the Nursing Home Five-Star Quality Rating System. This design was developed by CMS with assistance from Abt Associates, invaluable advice from leading researchers in the long-term care field who comprise the Technical Expert Panel (TEP) for this project, and numerous ideas contributed by consumer and provider groups. All of these organizations and groups have continued to contribute their input as the rating system has been refined and updated to incorporate newly available data. We believe the rating system offers valuable and comprehensible information to consumers based on the best data available. It features an Overall Quality Rating of one to five stars based on nursing home performance on three domains, each of which has its own rating (www.cms.gov).

Hold on a minute...

All this might look good on paper, but unless you are a nursing home insider or member of the Technical Expert Panel (TEP) there's really nothing simple about Care Compare so far. Further, there are reports of deep flaws in the new program that allow facilities to manipulate the data and skew the reports in their favor. More on this later. For additional understanding of the new system, here are the three domains:

Health Inspections - Measures based on outcomes from state health inspections: Ratings for the health inspections domain are based on the number, scope, and severity of deficiencies identified during the three most recent annual inspection surveys, as well as substantiated findings from the most recent 36 months of complaint investigations and focused infection control surveys. All deficiency findings are weighted by scope and severity. The health inspections rating also takes into account the number of revisits required to ensure that deficiencies identified during health inspection surveys have been corrected. • Staffing - Measures based on nursing home staffing levels: Ratings for the staffing domain are based on two measures: 1) Registered nurse (RN) hours per resident per day; and 2) total nurse (the sum of RN, licensed practical nurse (LPN), and nurse aide) hours per resident per day. Other types of nursing home staff, such as clerical or housekeeping staff, are not included in the staffing rating calculation. The staffing measures are derived from data submitted each quarter through the Payroll-Based Journal (PBJ) System, along with daily resident census derived from Minimum Data Set, Version 3.0 (MDS 3.0) assessments, and are case-mix adjusted based on the distribution of MDS 3.0 assessments by Resource Utilization Groups, version IV (RUG-IV groups). In addition to the overall staffing rating, a separate rating for RN staffing is also reported. • Quality Measures - Measures based on MDS and claims-based quality measures (QMs): Ratings for the quality measures are based on performance on 15 of the QMs that are currently posted on the Care Compare website. These include nine long-stay measures and six short-stay measures. Note that not all of the quality measures that are reported on Care Compare are included in the rating calculations. In addition to an overall quality of resident 1 Nursing Home Compare was retired on December 1, 2020 and replaced with Care Compare, which can be accessed at https://www.medicare.gov/care-compare/.　2 care rating, separate ratings for the quality of resident care for short-stay residents and longstay residents are also reported. In recognition of the multi-dimensional nature of nursing home quality, Care Compare displays ratings for each of these domains along with an overall rating. A companion document to this Technical Users' Guide (Nursing Home Compare–Five Star Quality Rating System: Technical Users' Guide–State-Level Cut Point Tables) provides the data for the state level cut points for the health inspection star ratings. The data table in the companion document is updated monthly. The cut points for the staffing ratings are included in Tables 3 and 4 in this Technical Users' Guide. Table 6 provides the cut points for the QM ratings, and the cut points for the individual QMs are in Appendix Table A2 (www.cms.gov).

Well, you get the picture.

The rating system is complex and peppered with specialized jargon. If consumers defer to the star ratings without further exploration of the data, it's easy to see how seniors and their loved ones might be misled. Worse yet, incomplete information provided by administrators can enhance a facility's overall score, creating the illusion of quality care where there is none.

New York Times investigative reporter Jessica Silver-Greenberg and data analyst Robert Gebeloff show how the MCS rating system has provided a badly distorted picture of the quality of care at the nation's nursing homes. "Many (facilities) relied on sleight-of-hand maneuvers to improve their ratings and hide shortcomings that contributed to the damage when the pandemic struck," the article states. "Payroll records provide the strongest evidence that, over the past decade, the government's rating system often exaggerated staffing levels, and rarely identified the periods of thin staffing that were common. Medicare is relying on the new data to evaluate staffing, but the updated system still hides the truth about which employees are working from day to day."

Even with more reliable data, Medicare's rating system is fundamentally flawed. Medicare still assigns stars by comparing care facilities to each other, essentially grading on a curve. As a result, many homes have kept their rating even when payroll records show lower staffing than before. To distill the results further, Medicare rated fewer than 1000 facilities, either because of data anomalies or because facilities were too new to provide reliable information. So far, there are no defined staffing levels for aides, allowing care facilities to make up the rules as they go along. Medicare has refused to set clearly defined standards, stating that it preferred the facilities to "make thoughtful, informed staffing plans based on need."

According to The New York Times, many top-ranked facilities receive high approval scores that do not reflect quality of care or conditions inside the building. While the five-star rating system has become the gold standard, it does not reveal what consumers need to know. Much of the information CMS receives from a facility is inaccurate and creates a higher, albeit erroneous rating. Some facilities inflate staffing levels by including aides who are on vacation, administrative leave, or by clocking in as an aide that doesn't exist. Homes with high ratings for quality of care may fail in-person inspections, but unless the agency follows up, the infraction is moot. Homes that know in advance about surprise inspections prepare by alerting staff and having facility data in order. In addition, inspectors who discover abuse and neglect may decide the infractions are minor, and not serious enough to document. It should come as no surprise that patients at 5-star facilities were just as likely to die of their illness as residents at the lowest rated homes.

At Cherry Tree Old Folks Home, aides discovered a way to manipulate data and outsmart the system, not with nefarious intent, but to survive chronic understaffing. Although pendant calls are documented and patient activity is logged electronically on a tablet, entries could be changed or deleted from the record if you knew what to click on. General information was routinely entered without seeing the patient. In aggregate, more time was devoted to the tablet than the resident.

My shift ended at 10:00 pm, but I rarely completed my work on time. At the height of the pandemic, care was provided by as few as two aides who were responsible for the entire building. Tasks like washing the dinner dishes and taking trash to the dumpster often had to wait, even if it meant staying late. The tablet, (officially called the POC or Point of Care), was inflexible, and would not allow new entries past 10:00 pm. Changing the clock in the settings menu became an essential skill that kept us in the administrant's good graces and allowed us to finish our work "on time," even when we were twenty minutes late.

Point Click Care (with its POC feature) is cloud-based technology designed to gather information about patients, their care, and their activity throughout the facility. While the system promises to improve quality and compliance, much of the company's online marketing focuses on making money. One headline states, "Track all services to *increase revenue per resident* while optimizing your occupancy by making more data-driven decisions." Also, PCC will "increase your bottom line, maximize reimbursement for services, and *increase financial results.*"

From pointclickcare.com: "Here are five tips and tricks to *driving revenue* with better resident assessments," and a testimonial that boasts, "12% revenue increase annually by leveraging insights from resident records." From the same article, "assessments are extremely important for driving improved *financial health*, as a better resident experience drives increased revenues."

While the administrant and his helpers were busy counting their money, I was sticking with my hypothesis that the leaders really were slow-witted Borg drones who lacked the capacity to understand right from wrong, but I had no evidence to prove it... at least not yet.

Diary of an Accidental Nursing Home Aide

Linda Lewis

Bram DeVries

Bram DeVries was a real estate developer, tall and gaunt, a victim of old age and cancer. He said he got lucky when he bought a large parcel of land cheap, just before a university began construction on 500 acres nearby. Knowing the students would need a place to live, Bram built 1000 apartment units, then another 500, and in the coming years, built 2000 more. He had been grossing $2 million a month in rent for decades, not including expenses, payroll, and capital improvements. He understood depreciation schedules and tax deductions like the back of his hand. Most of the students paid in cash; tax time must have been a doozie! Bram DeVries had homes in Boca Raton, Harbor Springs, Michigan, and a mansion on the Maumee River in Toledo. He was tall and dashing in his younger years, and now he needed help getting out of his chair.

"Hello, hello!" I bounded into his room with a big smile, genuinely happy to see him. "What's going on in here, my friend? Tell me something good!" He chuckled, as I took his thin hand in both of mine and gave it a squeeze. He felt so cold.

"Well, since you asked, I have a proposition for you…"

I helped him from his chair, to his walker, and to the men's room as the conversation continued.

"A proposition, eh? This sounds interesting… tell me more." Even at his advanced age, Mr. Devries was a flirt and probably a ladies' man back in the day.

"I would like to hire you to be my assistant. Four hours a day would be alright to start, more if you're available."

"You know I'd love to come work for you!"

"We could eat pizza, drink beer, and watch football on Saturdays," he offered, knowing we were both Buckeye fans.

"Mr. DeVries, did someone tell you I would work for beer and pizza?" I said it with feigned suspicion in my voice, knowing he would catch on.

"No," he chuckled, "but when I was younger, I never said no to an offer like that!" His comment made me think of an old friend, a boat mechanic named Drew Becker. I wondered what he was doing today and sighed.

"You'll have to clear it with the administrant," I said. "I don't think he likes me…"

"You probably ask too many questions," Mr. DeVries said, nodding. "He won't be a problem. He's not running the show around here anyway, you know that, right?" Bram's room was littered with newspapers, The Times, and The Wall Street Journal. He was more aware than most men half his age and knew what was going on in the world. I heard him reach for his walker and offered to assist. "I have plenty of money to pay you. I'll give you double what they're paying you here."

"My time is your time, sir. Whatever you can arrange, I'll be happy to help."

Diary of an Accidental Nursing Home Aide

Georgia

I dashed from his room, passed through the kitchen, drank some water, and ran to answer my next call. A coworker handed me a plate of roast turkey, mashed potatoes, and green beans. She said room 23 refused to eat, but I could try anyway. Georgia was classified non-verbal, but she always talked to me. The day we met, Georgia asked me why God wouldn't let her die. She was a century old and painfully alone. She regrated never having children, someone to cheer her. She was ready to move on.

"I don't know, my friend. Have you asked him?" I set up a tray table near her recliner and put down the plate.

"Asked who, for God's sake! You people ask too many damn questions."

"Asked God," I replied.

"Asked him what?"

"Why he won't let you die."

"Ah, hell... I don't know. What are we having for dinner?

When she talked, I cut up her food. When I talked, she chewed and swallowed. That's the way it was with us.

"How is your mother, dear? You said she had a brain tumor. She's coming here to live, isn't she?"

"She didn't make it, Georgia. She was just too sick and she died."

She reached for my hand as I offered her another bite."

"We got a call from the hospice nurse Sunday night. It was awful."

"You should take some time off. You have my deepest sympathies. If there's anything I can do..." She squeezed my hand; I adored her. From that day forward, all our conversations began the same way.

"Hello, hello! What's going on in here? Tell me something good!" I would say in my best Mary Poppins voice.

"Well, I'm still here, and that's good enough," she'd reply with a snort. "How are you, dear? How are you getting on without your mother? Would you like to talk?"

She was my friend; I was her confidant. We gave each other purpose.

"You know, when I was a young woman, I was quite a good bowler."

"A bowler?" The thought of Georgia in bowling shoes amused me and I giggled.

"My first husband, Carl… he had been in the Navy, you know…"

"I didn't know that." I replied.

"Oh, yes… and he was very handsome. Tall you know, and quite a good lover. I mean bowler… but not as good as me." I raised an eyebrow; she grinned.

He took me out every Wednesday. We played in a league with other young couples from the church. I was never athletic, as far as sports were concerned, but boy, could I throw that ball! Of course, I never took it seriously and never considered myself to be competitive. In those days women deferred to their husbands, so to beat them at any game would have been disrespectful, and I really did like Carl."

I knew from her file that her husband died twenty years ago, but his name was *Arthur.*

"Was Carl much older than you?" I was curious.

"Oh my, yes… nearly twenty years my senior. And he was rich! *Very rich!*" I glanced around the room at all the framed photos. There were three different pictures of Georgia in three different wedding gowns, with three different men!

"Well somebody has to marry the rich, right?" We roared like schoolgirls drunk on nostalgia. "Is this Carl?" I asked, handing her a picture from her nightstand. She was notably younger than the man in the photo. Her hair was done up in a victory roll; her makeup was masterfully applied.

"Men found that hairstyle very sexy, you know." I offered her a bite of turkey; she had a good appetite. "As a younger woman I always looked my best." She smoothed her white hair; the memory of Carl made her young again. Georgia had nearly finished her dinner and asked what we had for dessert. Unlike our first visit, she seemed less forgotten, more content. She just needed someone to listen— a surrogate granddaughter to hear her story. I went to the kitchen and returned with a nice piece of apple spice cake, one for her and one for me. I told her if she didn't stop talking I was going to eat both pieces! We laughed some more and ate up!

"Like I said," she went on, "I never took the game seriously. But on one Wednesday night, even after a few cocktails, I was bowling especially well. Our friends were taunting me, telling me this was the night I would bowl a perfect game. In case you're not familiar, dear, 300 is the highest score you can get. You have to bowl 12 strikes in a row, one strike in each of the first nine frames, and three more in the tenth frame."

A call came over the walkie. Bah, crackle, crackle... bah!! I couldn't understand a word, but I knew I had to go.

"Hold that thought, my friend." I gave her a sideways hug, took her empty plate, and headed for the kitchen to do the dishes.

Diary of an Accidental Nursing Home Aide

Dottie Dozier

There were residents at Cherry Tree Old Folks Home who were too big to move, even with a two person assist, so we used a Hoyer lift. A Hoyer is a small electric crane that provides a safe, if not somewhat awkward, way to move patients who have lost their mobility, but still need to be transferred from place to place. Some residents were terrified of being lifted in the canvas harness, while others enjoyed it so much they could not wait till next time! The machine has a sling bar and four attachment points where the harness hooks on. A remote control is used to open the machine's base wide enough to clear a wheelchair, or narrow enough to go under a bed. With patient swinging in mid-air, the Hoyer can also be rolled to a bedside commode or to the bathroom.

Diary of an Accidental Nursing Home Aide

A Hoyer Sit-to-Stand is for patients who still have some strength in their legs and can stabilize themselves on the machine's sturdy base. Its purpose is to transfer the patient safely from a wheelchair to the toilet, as well as their bed, a recliner, or a bedside commode. Because the lift is on wheels it provides safe transfers and mobility when nothing else can.

One of my favor residents at Cherry Tree was a great big gal named Dottie, short for Dorothy. She was a retired high school principal who moved here from California to be closer to her kids. Her mind was sharp, but her body was failing. Like most widows she missed her husband fiercely, but had peace knowing she would see him again someday. Despite her health issues and grief, Dottie enjoyed a good meal and always had delicious snacks on hand whenever I stopped by for a visit. We were sisters in Christ and loved sharing our mutual stories of salvation.

When there were still enough workers, before COVID-19 robbed the long-term care workforce, I followed a coworker to Dottie's room to assist with the Hoyer, which had to be managed with two people.

"Joo did already have a BM?" asked my coworker.

"No," Dottie replied. "I tried but I can't go."

"No, that is no good. Joo must go."

"I can't go."

"But joo must. Joo must try."

"I did try… I really did, but I can't."

"No, that is no good."

"If there was any way I could sit on the toilet, I think I could go…" She was pleading.

Where else could she possibly go if not the toilet? I wondered. *If not the toilet, then where?*

"Joo have to go in your diaper. Just sit here and go." Dottie was in her wheelchair looking at me. I wanted to help, to make this right, but how? "Joo have to go. I'll be back in 15 minutes."

A Hoyer lift harness is available with a hole in the canvas. It is designed to allow someone to use a toilet once they've been lowered to the right position. While I was no expert, I was certain of two things: One, the appropriate harness was available on Amazon for under $200, and two, no one in any care facility should be required to poop in their pants.

I found the administrant sitting in his office behind a pile of papers talking on his cell phone.

"Are you aware that Dottie Dozier is being forced to have a bowel movement in her diaper instead of using the toilet?"

"Dozier… Dozier… ummm."

"Room 21."

"Dorothy in Room 21." He typed something into his computer and looked at the screen. "Well, that can't be right. It says right here that Room 21 is independent for using the bathroom…"

"She *was* independent nine months ago, before she fell and broke her hip. She's in a wheelchair now and she weighs 300 pounds."

"Rats. I guess I should have known that." He picked up a tall stack of papers and fumbled through them, as if locating a certain document would make pooping in a diaper okay.

The administrant folded his hands and leaned back in his chair. "What can I do to help," he said in a flat tone, his eyes avoiding the angry look on my face.

"She needs a Hoyer harness with a whole in the middle so she can use the toilet and not poop in her pants."

The administrant twisted up his face and shook his head. "Gosh, Room 21 is on hospice, and there's a form we have to complete and fax to their administrant, and tomorrow is Saturday, and I know they don't work on the weekend.

"It's $200 on Amazon."

"Well, let me just see…"

He picked up the phone and pretended to dial. "Yes, hello… Miss Yvette?" I was thinking about a sketch on the old Carol Burnett show where Mr. Tudball calls his secretary, Mrs. Ah-huh-Wiggins, but she doesn't know how to use the intercom.

"Yes, I'm here in my office with Linda and she would like us to order a special harness for Room 21. I realize she is on hospice and they don't work on the weekends but it's okay with me if you want to order it anyway. Just fill out the special form. Well, okay, Miss Yvette. That is all for now. Bye bye."

I never found out if Dottie got the harness she needed. I was never scheduled to work in that part of the building again.

Diary of an Accidental Nursing Home Aide

Jack

The clock was ticking; I had to keep moving. Everyone wanted to talk, to tell their stories, but there was only one of me to go around. I was now working through all my breaks, and still trying to make time to spend with my residents.

"Hey, I never got to tell you what happened after I bought the station wagon! Do you have a minute?" Jack saw me pass by in the hallway. I was already way behind.

"Of course I do!" I picked up his lunch plate, set it aside, and poured him a fresh drink of water. "I knew there had to be more to this story!" I dusted the furniture and cleaned his bathroom as I listened.

"Well, I had a few alternatives, most of them not good." Jack was seated in his recliner. He seemed more tired than usual. "In 1972 Ford Motor Company put out some real bad products— the Pinto and the Maverick."

"Please tell me you didn't buy a Maverick!!"

"Hell, no! Both cars were in response to the energy crisis and couldn't get out of their own way." I laughed out loud. All old men who loved cars sounded exactly alike. "I picked up a nice used Galaxy 500 that came in on trade... just 7000 miles. The price was right, and that gave me something decent to drive until I bought my first Thunderbird, a 1975. From that day on, I was a T-bird man through-and-through, and bought a new car every couple years."

Jack didn't look his age. I could picture him behind the wheel, and collecting trophies at the local car shows.

"I retired from selling cars after 25 years. It was a good run. I had made the dealership and myself a lot of money. They gave me a real nice bonus on my last day, and do you know what I did with it?"

He had a photo in his hand. "I bet I can guess!"

"An old timer at New Boston had a red 1957 T-Bird. Whenever he came by for coffee and donuts, back when I was selling cars to the workers, I said to him, "George, one of these days you're gonna get tired of that car and I'm gonna buy it from you." We always laughed, but when I retired, that's exactly what I did! That car won best of show everywhere we went."

"What a fantastic story! Do you still have the car?" He looked down at his hands and was quiet.

"Wish I did… miss her like crazy, but we had to sell the car to help pay for this place." I felt bad for him. Growing old is very expensive, and I wouldn't want to be here, either.

My pager was blaring. "I have to run, Jack. Oh, and by the way, my husband and I just bought a 1964 Thunderbird."

"Oh you did, did you?" He perked up a bit.

"Vintage burgundy with a Landau top. Picked her up last night. Came from a man up in Cambridge… an old timer with quite a collection." A smile crossed his face like a ray of sunshine. But he was coughing more than usual. I offered him some water.

"A man name of Jim? Lives in a big, fancy house just outside of town with a four-car garage and a weathervane on top?" I raised an eyebrow. "I knew him well. What did you have to give for the car?"

"He was asking 12, he took 10.

"Fourth generation… I bet she's a beauty."

"You know, I'm off tomorrow. Maybe we could swing by so you could have a look," I suggested.

"I would love nothing more!"

"What time is good?"

"I've got all the time in the world," he replied. I thought so, too.

I checked with the front desk to make sure 1:00 was okay. The residents would be finished with lunch by then. The next morning the receptionist called. "I'm afraid we need to cancel your meeting with Jack. He passed away last night in his sleep. He had COVID-19.

Linda Lewis

Bram DeVries

"The administrant said I can have you for two hours today, so we better get to work." Mr. DeVries was waiting for me with a long hand-written list on the tray table in front of him. "There were stacks of unopened mail on his nightstand, and boxes of mail on the floor. A tall file cabinet had drawers half open with stacks of mail inside. He explained that he had gotten so far behind with his business dealings due to his illness, and now he wondered how he would ever catch up. "Do you think you could help me with that?"

I gathered empty boxes from the kitchen, and a Sharpie from Miss Yvette's desk. I took a huge trash can from Housekeeping. Though he never complained, I saw pain in his face, his brow deeply furrowed. I paged a nurse, expecting no one to come. I was trying to stay in my lane as Miss Yvette insisted, but that got harder after Jack died. I was not just providing care and comfort to the residents; I was guarding my own heart as well. I wanted to roll back time and heal everyone who got sick. I wanted my mom to be healthy and alive again. It was too much death for me to bear.

I reposition Mr. DeVries in his lift chair recliner, and offered him a pack of Fig Newtons. The foam padding was flattened and hard from months of continuous use, and the remote control only worked half the time. When I asked the administrant about replacing it with something more comfortable, he twisted up his face and shook his head. "Gosh, Room 26 is on hospice, and there's a form we have to complete and fax to their administrant, and tomorrow is Saturday, and I know they don't work on the weekend."

"My father worked as a salesman at the Howard Miller Clock Company in Holland, Michigan," he began, as I poured him a drink of water and lifted a box of mail onto his bed. "I was the youngest of six, and there was no one to look after me during the summers, so I went to work with my father. I swept, and cleaned, and ran errands for Mr. Miller, who began paying me a small wage. As I got older and advanced through the grades, he took me under his wing, so to speak. When the Depression hit, he diversified the clock business by adding a furniture division. I went with him to the Century of Progress Exposition in Chicago where I met his business partners who were investing in the new line. The furniture division turned out to be a huge success and got us through the worst economic crisis in the nation's history.

"That is quite a story... you should have written a book!"

"Well, there's more." I adjusted the cushions on his chair; he grimaced and moaned. The nurse never came.

"My father was very conservative. He was a product of his day, and had a lot on his plate supporting our large family. I never told him where I got the money to purchase the land that made me a fortune because he might not have approved."

I was opening mail and sorting through a lot of financial information, documents he may have wanted to keep private. "What about the brokerage accounts?"

"If I didn't trust you completely, you wouldn't be here," he said, as if reading my mind. "Just save the monthly statements, make sure they're labelled, and put them in a box. I'll time to go over them later."

I put a rubber band around the envelopes, picked up another box, and continued sorting. "I'm all ears, Mr. DeVries. What happened next?"

"Well, Mr. Miller said he liked my work ethic... said I had a bright future and asked me to manage the new furniture division. It was a huge opportunity for a young man straight out of high school, especially when families were struggling and there were no jobs to be had."

"The Depression."

"Yes. It was a terrible time. But every now and again those fellas from the Chicago Exposition came down and met with Mr. Miller about business matters, then went out for a drink of whiskey. When I was of legal age, they invited me to join them."

"What do you want me to do with the magazines?" I interjected.

"Go ahead and pitch 'em."

He continued. "The men were a curious sort. They weren't flashy like other men in those days who had money, but instead went around in Carhartt jackets and broken-down boots, almost as if they didn't want to be noticed."

"I know the type,' recalling a man I once knew.

"The men spent their weekends at a private club up in Manistee... finest duck hunting in all of Michigan! The senior of the two used to say they must pay the waterfowl to light there just so he could shoot 'em. It was expensive to join, and nearly impossible to get in."

"There was a young Russian who helped his father in the kitchen, a boy named Sergei... a disagreeable youth if there ever was one. It's true he made the best duck and goose sauce in the county... couldn't complain about that. Trouble is, he never washed his hands after he went to the bathroom! We never knew if we were going to die of the typhoid on the ride home, or live to see another day!"

I imagined a supply closet at the club in Manistee... well stocked, but no key.

"And here's another thing." He lowered his voice to a whisper. "I can tell you for a fact the young Sergei used to swing both ways, if you know what I mean. You wouldn't think that a bunch of men with guns would be into that sort of thing. We just kept our distance, except for the duck and goose sauce, of course. Mr. Goodhart always locked his door when we stayed for the weekend... wanted no part of it.

"Mr. Goodhart?"

"Why yes... Clarence Goodhart and his friend, man name of Becker. They were the investors in the Miller furniture line, and that's who loaned me the money for the land. Did the whole deal on a handshake.

"So you developed your properties and went on to become very rich... and what happened to those men?"

"Last I heard they ran into some trouble with the law... may have done some time, but who can be sure."

I had a million questions to ask him but there was never enough time. As I was cleaning out the last file, a lady came in carrying her lunch box, a coat, and stack of magazines. "I'm Mr. DeVries's private duty nurse. His family hired me to sit with him until... *well, you know.*"

I got a lump in my throat. Not sure I'd ever see him again or hear how his story ended, I squeezed his hand and said goodbye.

Diary of an Accidental Nursing Home Aide

Linda Lewis

Georgia

I had thirty minutes before I had to clock in and start my shift. I passed by Georgia's room and peeked inside. She was supposed to pick up her story where we left off, the part about how she met her second husband. But instead, she was in bed asleep, with an oxygen cannula and a tank beside her bed. I took her hand in mine, then looked at the tablet to see her vitals. She did not have a temperature when Patriciana made her rounds in the morning, but I noted she hadn't eaten anything or been to the bathroom all day. I scanned her room for clues as to what might be going on. There was a warm bottle of

Diary of an Accidental Nursing Home Aide

Ensure on her nightstand, unopened, and next to that, an open pack of tiny disposable mouth sponges on a stick, sort of like a Q-tip. I learned about these as a hospice volunteer. You dip them in cool water and allow the patient to suck the moisture from the sponge, or swish it around their mouth and cheeks to help with dryness. The sight of these products was a very bad sign. I felt like I'd been hit by a train.

I tried to maintain my composure. I leaned in and smiled; her eyes fluttered a bit. "I brought you something, my friend... it's me, Linda." Her eyes flew open!

"Ahh, heck. And here I thought God was going to let me die in peace." She tried to laugh but coughed instead. Her voice was barely audible, but her sense of humor remained. "What's in your bag? Didn't I say, 'no gifts?' I held her hand and placed it against my cheek. It was so cold, and her fingertips were already turning blue. Another bad sign." I really just wanted to cry and ask her not to go. As far as wonderful old women in my life, she was all I had left.

Instead, I reached in my bag and pulled out an antique bowling pin, vintage 1950. I knew she regretted having to leave her trophy behind when she moved to Cherry Tree. I had painted her name on it in gold leaf, then outlined the letters in black with the number '300' at the bottom, imagining that's what the original might have looked like. I gave her a sip of water from a sponge. She nodded, then dozed off again.

I raced through my duties, taking temperatures, recording them on the tablet, and making sure everyone in my section was dry and comfortable. I wiped down the countertops and appliances with the cleaner that I brought from home, then set the dining room tables for dinner. I brought pitchers of juice and water from the kitchen, and turned on the food warmers. I had just enough time to run to see Georgia before serving dinner.

The sun had set, and the lights were dim. I asked a nurse about her condition, but she barely spoke English and stuttered when she tried. I heard a faint rattle before I reached Georgia's bedside. The death rattle is a distinctive sound a person makes as their life is coming to a close. It happens when they can no longer swallow or cough effectively. It is a terrible sound and difficult for loved ones to hear. And I was her loved one. Her bowling pin trophy sat on the nightstand. I pulled down my mask so I could wipe my nose and cry. My pager went off. It was time to move the residents to the dining room for dinner and I had to go. I stroked her hair and whispered; *I'll be back…*

Diary of an Accidental Nursing Home Aide

I cleared the tables, brought out dessert, and made coffee, then scraped the plates and threw away the pans of food that didn't get eaten. The residents who were more independent sat in the living room watching TV, while I took the others to the bathroom, put on their pajamas, and tucked them into bed. Everyone was where they were supposed to be, safe and sound, occupied or sleeping. My shift was over at 10:00 pm. I went to see Georgia.

She was resting on her side, facing away from the door. Had someone repositioned her? Had a hospice nurse arrived to help? I stepped quietly around her bed. Her jaw was slack, and her mouth had a look of surprise. Her eyes were wide open and bulging. One of Georgia's arms was erect and reaching toward the window, a sign that rigor mortis had already set in.

In my first week of training as a hospice volunteer in Boca Raton, Florida, we read from a book by Kathy Kalina called, Midwife of Souls.

"We are eyewitnesses to the infinite value of the last days. We see the miraculous spiritual growth and reconciliations, the heroism, humor, and unconditional love of the dying. We feel the graces that flow…"

One of the top fears that is universal across many cultures concerning death, is the fear of dying alone. But with hospice being short staffed due to COVID-19, and Cherry Tree experiencing a staffing shortage as well, Georgia died alone. I should have been there.

I closed her eyes and stroked her cheek, as I waited for a hospice nurse to arrive and take over. Silently I prayed, thanking God for the opportunity to be her friend, if only for a short while, then sang some verses of Amazing Grace. The hospice nurse was on the phone outside her door, making arrangements to remove her body from the building.

Diary of an Accidental Nursing Home Aide

Linda Lewis

Sophie

One of my first patients in Boca was an old, grouchy woman named Sophie, 105 years young, who was a former New York socialite and the widow of a famous baseball player. She was the author of several children's books, one of which is still popular today, and suggested I would be a writer someday, too. The mother of only one son, Myron was 80 years old and suffering from Alzheimer's Disease. His photo was on her nightstand; he didn't know his mother.

It was late at night when I got the call. When I arrived, Sophie was sleeping but still conscious. She demanded a cigarette, and snarled when I wouldn't comply. It was her eleventh hour and she still had spark. I sat at her bedside riffling through my notes, looking for the number to call for a nurse, when her eyes flew open! She sat up in bed, looking toward the doorway, and extended her arms. With a final surge of energy, she cried, "Hemis, Hemis!" Her voice was clear and her face was radiant. It was the most joyous moment in our time together. Through the years, Sophie defeated practically every kind of cancer, but now it was her time to go. The next morning I got a call from the social worker for an update and to complete some forms. I mentioned Sophie's last words and repeated, 'Hemis, Hemis.' The woman was quiet for a moment, then said, '*Hamish.*" Hamish was her youngest son. He died of scarlet fever when he was a baby. She asked whether Sophie had ever talked about him. I said, she didn't have to, he was with her last night.

I wondered if Georgia was reaching out for someone... perhaps Carl, or a baby she never met.

Linda Lewis

June

I had one more resident to see before I left Cherry Tree that night. June was a former member of the Radio City Music Hall Rockettes, now crippled with arthritis, and living the last season of her life all alone. She adored me and the feeling was mutual. June had already read my first book, *Seeking Miranda*, and was halfway through the second. I helped her to the ladies' room, then into her pajamas. They were smooth black polyester with a collar, cuffs, and rhinestone buttons down the front. The matching bed jacket had a detachable feather boa, and a tag that said Jacobson's.

"June, these are fabulous!" I exclaimed, wishing I had a pair. "Look at all this sparkle and fizz!"

"Ha!" she chortled. "Now you sound just like Miranda!" I blushed and turned down her covers. "She seemed like a nice enough girl, good intentions and all, but so foolish and misguided!"

"But I'm not Miranda. A lot of people ask me that, and I'm really not her."

"It's okay, my dear. We've all made mistakes. Miranda just made more than most." I appreciated her incite and candor. (*I really am Miranda.*) "I'm delighted things turned out well for you." I wondered when I would see her again. I never even got to hear her story; I bet it was a doozie.

I lifted her into bed— she was too weak to pivot— then poured a fresh glass of water for her nightstand. A box of Kleenex and the remote were within reach. I leaned forward to reposition her higher on her pillow so she could watch TV. She seemed so heavy. She should have been a two person assist. I felt a snap. I was always sore at the end of my shift because the work was so physically demanding, but this was different. The next morning, I couldn't get out of bed, and learned at the emergency room that I had sprained the lumbar and thoracic regions of my back when I moved her. I spent the next twelve weeks going to physical therapy and writing a book.

As I left Cherry Tree that night, I saw Neil Lipman coming out of the supply closet. He looked surprisingly refreshed for a fat, bearded chain smoker who lived on beer and chicken wings. A shiny, gold key fell from his pocket, but he kept on walking. It was the only mystery I hadn't solved during my time at the facility, so I unlocked the door and stepped inside.

The supply closet was dark, illuminated only by a soft green glow. I paused and waited for my eyes to adjust, careful not to bump into anything and give myself away. The space appeared much larger than I expected, with shelves on either side, and a row of tall, narrow machines that lined the back wall. Through a window I could see the lights of the llama farm in the distance.

Each structure had an alcove slightly larger than a human form, with a panel of vertical lights in the center, and a grouping of smaller lights to the left. There were gears and connectors that gave the machines an ominous look.

I spotted Helga standing silently in one of the chambers, her arm resting on a narrow platform at chest level. Tim and I had authoritative knowledge of all things Star Trek after rewatching every episode during the pandemic. I knew at once Helga was standing in a Borg regeneration alcove. Judging by the pulsating green and white lights, she was completing her regeneration cycle, a process that connects the drone with the mother ship, transfers data, and ensures the Borg cannot think for itself. I left Helga without saying a word. It's not likely she would have responded anyway.

I hurried out of the supply closet, past cases of adult diapers, laundry detergent, and Super Clean Flushable Wipes, then slipped through the door and closed it behind me. I was holding the elusive key. Without access to the supply room and regular regeneration, the leaders would eventually return to their fully human state and be faced with the mess they had created.

I dropped the key in the zipper pocket of my Vera Bradley tote bag and walked in the dark to my car. These were the days of life and death during COVID-19, a time I would never forget.

Diary of an Accidental Nursing Home Aide

Christel

I was resting on a heating pad when the phone rang. I didn't recognize the area code. I usually ignore every call that's not familiar, but this time I picked up. It was a police officer from Boulder, Colorado. My brother Tom had passed away that evening. He gave me the name of the mortuary where his body was taken, and expressed his condolences; it was all the information he had. My mother needed her son in heaven, more than the people of earth needed him here.

Tommy walked into choir practice, his old gig bag in one hand, a boloney sandwich in the other. His hair was tousled; he was five minutes late. His old trumpet, the one that had survived middle school concerts, marching band, and late nights with his musician friends, was no longer dented and scuffed, but bright as the heavenly realms, ready to play for the glory of God. My mom was distracted. She looked like the college girl in the photos I found at her condo, lovely and beaming, but with more peace than before. The choir director tapped the podium with his baton. Someone was still talking; it was my mom. She handed a new friend a satin drawstring pouch with a carnelian bracelet inside, and offered to teach her German. Even though she had only been in heaven a few months, she already knew everyone's birthday and was busy making jewelry.

The organist played the introduction to a traditional Easter hymn, Only God himself could anticipate what would happen next.

> "Crown him the Lord of life
> Who triumphed o'er the grave,
> And rose victorious in the strife
> For those he came to save;
> His glories now we sing
> Who died and rose on high,
> Who died eternal life to bring,
> And lives that death may die."

My mom recognized a familiar countermelody, just the way he always played it. Tommy came to see her after all, and this time their reunion would be eternal.

Diary of an Accidental Nursing Home Aide

Linda Lewis

Diary of an Accidental Nursing Home Aide

References

Campbell, Stephen. "Quality Care through Quality Jobs." Paraprofessional Healthcare Institute, Feb. 2018, www.phinational.org.

Center for Medicare and Medicaid Services. "Design for Care Compare Nursing Homes Five-Star Quality Rating System," Jan. 2021, www.cms.gov/Medicare/Provider-Enrollment-and Certification/CertificationandComplianc/Downloads/usersguide .pdf

Meyer, Harris. "Nursing Homes' Flawed Business Model Worsens COVID Crisis." AARP the Magazine, 7 Dec. 2020, www.aarp.org.

Silver-Greenberg, Jessica and Gebeloff, Robert. "Covid Forces Families to Rethink Nursing Home Care." The New York Times, 8 May 2021, www.nytimes.com

Silver-Greenberg, Jessica and Gebeloff, Robert. "Maggots, Rape, and Yet Five Stars: How U.S. Ratings of Nursing Homes Mislead the Public." The New York Times, 13 Mar. 2021, www. nytimes.com.

Span, Paula. "Some Assisted-Living Residents Don't Get Promised Care, Suit Charges, Court decisions in California may shed light on how large nursing home chains make staffing decisions." The New York Times, 14 Feb. 2020, www.nytimes.com.

Thomas, Katie. "Medicare Star Ratings Allow Nursing Homes to Game the System." The New York Times, 24 Aug. 2014, www.nytimes.com.

Linda Lewis

"UNITED STATES DISTRICT COURT Northern District of California AUDREY HEREDIA, as successor-in-interest to the Estate of Carlos Heredia; and CORBINA MANCUSO as successor in interest to the Estate of Ruby Mancuso; on their own behalves and on behalf of others similarly situated." Senior Justice Law Firm, 27 June 2017, www. seniorjustice. com.

Zallman, Leah et al. "Care for America's Elderly and Disabled People Relies on Immigrant Labor." Health Affairs, June 2019, www.healthaffairs.org.

Diary of an Accidental Nursing Home Aide

Made in the USA
Monee, IL
11 July 2021

73399310R00115